Sm61h

HEART OF VALOR

By the same author

The Night of the Solstice

L ˙ J ˙ S M I T H

HEART of VALOR

▼ ▼ ▼

MACMILLAN PUBLISHING COMPANY
New York

COLLIER MACMILLAN CANADA
Toronto

MAXWELL MACMILLAN INTERNATIONAL PUBLISHING GROUP
New York Oxford Singapore Sydney

Macmillan Publishing Company
866 Third Avenue, New York, NY 10022
Collier Macmillan Canada, Inc.
1200 Eglinton Avenue East
Suite 200
Don Mills, Ontario M3C 3N1
First Edition   Printed in the United States of America

10 9 8 7 6 5 4 3 2 1

The text of this book is set in 12 point Electra.

Library of Congress Cataloging-in-Publication Data
Smith, L. J. (Lisa J.)
Heart of valor / by L. J. Smith.—1st ed.   p.   cm.
Summary: When their friend, sorceress Morgana Shee, embarks on a
mission to recover the Heart of Valor, a ruby giving the possessor
almost limitless power, four children already in serious danger
pursue her to offer their help. Sequel to "Night of the Solstice."
ISBN 0-02-785861-8
[1. Fantasy. 2. Brothers and sisters—Fiction.] I. Title.
PZ7.S6537He 1990 [Fic]—dc20   90-5827 CIP   AC

To my parents,
whose love, support, and example
have helped me find my dreams

CONTENTS

▼ ▼ ▼

ONE

▾ ▾ ▾

Claudia Sends a Letter . . .

Claudia Hodges-Bradley twisted a strand of mouse brown hair around her fingers and frowned mightily, trying to concentrate on Mrs. Anderson's review of this week's spelling words. There would be a test this afternoon, and Mrs. Anderson's tests always gave Claudia stomach cramps. She knew she needed to pay attention . . . but she would rather just listen to the birds.

Not that birds, in general, had a great deal to say for themselves. They could sit happily for hours shrieking, "I'm a bluejay! I'm a bluejay! This is *my* tree! This is *my* tree!" So it wasn't that they were very interesting, just much more interesting than school or Mrs. Anderson.

At a steely glance from that lady Claudia jumped guiltily and stopped twisting her hair. Mrs. Anderson disapproved of hair twisting, pencil chewing, and nail biting, all of which Claudia seemed to be doing more of this year than ever before. Claudia was a square, serious child, whose blue eyes always looked a little anxious in class pictures. This year they usually seemed to look that way in the mirror, too.

Since she couldn't twist her hair, she put a hand to her chest to feel the comforting bump of the charm beneath her shirt. It was so familiar she could see it with her fingers: the broad crescent of silver from which hung three stones: sardonyx, black opal, and bloodstone, each inscribed with spidery writing in the language of the Wildworld. Claudia couldn't read any of the symbols on the stones, but she understood very well what the charm did. It enabled her to talk to animals.

Perhaps *communicate* was a better word than *talk*. Animal language depended as much on body movement—the tilt of a head, the flip of a wing, the quirk of a tail—as it did on mere sounds. Except when the message was meant to be heard and understood over long distances, like the killdeer outside daring anyone to come close to *her* nest. . . .

Claudia sucked in her breath sharply. The killdeer had been saying something quite different for several minutes now, and Claudia had just realized what it was. Automatically, she started to raise her hand to tell Mrs. Anderson, then hastily snatched the hand down again. The teacher would think she had gone crazy. Better just to wait it out. After all, there was nothing Mrs. Anderson could do about it. And maybe—Claudia brightened considerably—they wouldn't get to the spelling test this afternoon.

And then her breath stopped, and her heart underneath the silver charm began to pound violently. Because it was the last week of April and the spring canned-food drive was almost over, and Mrs. Anderson's class was winning. And the tower they had made with their 246 (as of this morning) cans of food rose high in all its symmetrical splendor against the wall on one side of the room.

Claudia could just see it out of the corner of her eye without turning her head. Remmy Garcia was sitting a foot or so away from it. Claudia liked Remmy. He kept white rats at home. She didn't much like Beth Ann, who sat behind him, but as her sister Alys would say, that was beside the point.

"Claudia!"

Claudia started. She had twisted around in her seat to look at the cans; now she turned her agonized gaze back on Mrs. Anderson.

"Claudia, if you want to stare at your little friend, recess is the time to do it—except that you just lost five minutes of your recess. Do you understand?"

Claudia scarcely heard the titters of the class. She had to do something to stop what was going to happen, but she had not the first idea what. Even Alys, who was a junior in high school and could fix almost anything, couldn't fix something like this. But still, she felt a strong compulsion to tell Alys. . . . No. Not Alys. *Janie.*

Janie might be able to help. Janie did all sorts of strange things these days. Most of them were of no use whatsoever, but some were. Feverishly, Claudia began rummaging in her desk for pencil and paper. She would write a letter to Janie.

"Claudia! Claudia Hodges-Bradley!" Claudia dropped the pencil. Mrs. Anderson was staring as though she couldn't believe her eyes.

"Claudia, if you would just learn to pay attention, school wouldn't be so difficult for you. Now you've lost *ten* minutes of recess."

As the teacher turned back to the blackboard Claudia stealthily picked up the pencil again. She would have to be very careful; if she lost the last five minutes of recess she would have no way of sending the letter. She wrote with her eyes glued to Mrs. Anderson's back, only snatching a peek at the paper now and then. Writing was hard work for Claudia under any circumstances, and spelling a hopeless task even when she wasn't rattled. Letters seemed to have a life of their own, jumping in and out of words and turning themselves upside down. When the note was finished she surveyed it doubtfully. She felt almost certain *towwer* was misspelled. But Janie was very smart, she told herself comfortingly. Janie would understand.

The recess bell rang. Claudia sat for ten minutes under the forbidding eye of Mrs. Anderson, trying not to twist her hair.

Dismissed at last, she burst out onto the blacktop already scanning the perimeter of the playground. There were lots of dogs in Villa Park and usually one or two could be seen gamboling on the other side of the chain-link fence. Yes— there! But it was so far away, on the other side of the big kids' playground.

Claudia, a third grader, was not allowed on that playground. She didn't know what they did to you if they caught you there—possibly suspended you as they had suspended Tony Stowers for hitting another little boy over the head with a bag of marbles. Probably sent you to the principal. She cast a glance at the teacher on yard duty, saw he was looking the other way, and began to slink.

She felt horribly exposed, the only child on an endless field of forbidden grass, and when she reached the fence she hunkered down, making herself as small as possible. She whistled. The dog, a sort of setter-spaniel mix with something vaguely Airedale about the ears, stopped scratching itself and looked surprised. It recovered quickly and trotted over, wagging its whole body and uttering short, sharp barks in an attempt to tell her how eager it was to do whatever she wanted it to do, how proud it was to have been chosen to do it, how valiantly it would try to accomplish the task, how—

"Be quiet," said Claudia, desperately. The dog groveled. "I need you to help me. You know who I am?"

The setter rolled eyes like chocolate drops expressively. Everyone knew Claudia.

"All right, well, I've got a sister—not my biggest sister, Alys, but the other one, Janie. She goes to the junior high school—the place across the street with lots of kids. You know that place?"

The setter knew it perfectly. Pizza in the cafeteria trash cans, rats under the Quonset huts, and gophers in the field. A wonderful place.

"Well, I need you to go there and find Janie and give her this note. Janie is—" Claudia stopped, overwhelmed by the task of trying to describe Janie in terms the setter would understand.

The dog raised its head off its paws and barked once, wriggling in delight. It knew Janie, too. Threw away half her lunch and smelled like magic. Nothing easier than to find her.

"Oh, thank you!" said Claudia, pushing her hand through a diamond of the chain-link to touch its wet nose. Then she carefully folded the note and poked it through.

"Now, go! Please hurry." As the dog trotted away, letter in its teeth, tail high, pride in its commission showing in

every line of its body, the bell rang again. Recess was over.
And Claudia was an ocean of grass away from her rightful place. Her only hope was to hug the older kids' classrooms and get back to her room through the middle of the school.

There was, she discovered at once, a fatal flaw in this plan. Barring the way between the intermediate and the primary wings of the school was a chain-link gate. It was not locked, but Claudia knew she would never have the courage to touch it, much less open it. Besides, there was a teacher on the other side—her year-before-last-year's teacher, Mr. Pigeon.

Mr. Pigeon had been a nice teacher. He had never made her name sound like "Clod-ia" or told her her writing looked like chicken tracks or her attitude was terrible. His class motto had been "All for one and one for all." Claudia sniffled as she turned to go the other way.

Mr. Pigeon heard. He turned around, surprised.

"Claudia, what—?" But instead of finishing the question he looked hard at her face. Then he put a finger to his lips and opened the gate, beckoning her through.

"All for one . . ." he whispered, as she looked up at him in dumb gratitude. "Better hurry. But don't run!"

Claudia walked until she was out of eyeshot, then galloped. She managed to slide into her chair just as Mrs. Anderson turned around to announce a spelling test. And then there was nothing to do but sit, pencil clutched in her fist, stomach aching, unable to ignore the killdeer outside. It was shrieking the same thing as before, over and over:

"Earthquake! Earthquake!

"Ground move, ground shake!"

From somewhere a chaffinch added a note in counter-point: "Take wing! Take wing!"

Claudia wished she could. It was all up to Janie now.

T W O
▾ ▾ ▾
. . . And Janie Receives It

I'd like a volunteer to tell us the answer to the last two equations here . . . Janie Hodges-Bradley."

Janie, who had not volunteered, looked up from her eighth-grade algebra textbook, blinked, and scanned the blackboard quickly, once. "X equals seven or negative seven, y equals thirteen or negative thirteen."

Mr. Lambert pursed his lips, tapped the chalk once or twice on the board, and spread his free hand in a sort of grudging shrug. "Correct," he said, and he and Janie exchanged a glance. He knew she was reading another book behind her text, and it grieved him, but as long as she knew the answers he would let her get away with it. He might have been surprised—and much less aggrieved—if he had known that the book was *Modern Trigonometry*. There were a surprisingly large number of calculations to be done in magic.

This was the first year Janie had been glad of her mother's refusal to let her skip a grade or three when the elementary school had wanted it so long ago. Because if she studied calculus during algebra period, German and Latin during Spanish, herb lore during history, metamorphic petrology during art, and the collected writings of Darion the Falcrister during literature; and stayed up late every night, she could just about get through the course of study Morgana Shee had set for her. Just about. It wasn't easy, but it was possible.

Janie bent her head once more over her books. She was only alerted to the presence of the dog by the stifled giggles and hisses of the other students. When she noticed it, it was just finishing a quick circuit of the room and heading straight for her as if it had known her all its life. Reaching her, it planted muddy front paws on her lap and thrust its head against her chest, nearly knocking her out of her seat. Then it raised its head and barked once, joyously, in her face.

"Look," said someone, mildly. "Janie Hodges-Bradley has a dog."

Two seats away, Bliss Bascomb turned a silvery blond head. "Janie Hodges-Bradley *is* a dog," she whispered, and there was laughter, and then Mr. Lambert intervened.

"Someone remove that animal," he said, waving an eraser dismissively.

Janie sat with her hands pressed on her knees as the dog was dragged away. She did this partly to quell the desire to do violence to Bliss Bascomb, and partly because of what no one else had seen: the dog had deposited a small, wet wad of paper in her lap. When everyone's attention was safely on the lesson again she unfolded the paper.

After studying it for several minutes she rubbed her eyes, and tried again. The note had suffered considerably since Claudia had written it. It looked as if it had been dropped once or twice in the gutter, and parts of the paper were entirely disintegrated by canine saliva. What was left of the writing bore a pronounced resemblance to chicken tracks. "Deere Janie," "drids," and "rthkwack" were about all she could make out.

Although the signature had been obliterated she had no doubt as to the author. For one thing, it was on elementary-school paper, the kind with the three big lines; and for another, who else would send a letter via dog? And Claudia must have thought it was important, because she knew Janie would hate to be interrupted at school.

For a moment Janie was tempted to ignore the whole thing; pretend she hadn't got the letter, or that she had thought it was a joke. A year before, she would certainly have done this. But now . . . well, she was annoyed with Claudia, but she couldn't just let it rest. There was some kind of trouble afoot.

Janie sighed, eyed the students around her surreptitiously, and reached down to unzip her backpack.

She drew out a stick. It was rowan, exactly as long as the distance between the tips of her fingers and the crook of her elbow, and sanded to a finish like satin. It had been hollowed out and filled with cinquefoil, agrimony, and other herbs. To this had been added a rolled-up parchment on which Morgana Shee had written in the language of Findahl, the Wildworld, and a piece of white cotton stained with three drops of Janie's blood and three drops of Morgana's. It was a virtue wand, drawing power from the Gold Staff of the sorceress to the hand of her apprentice.

But it had never been intended to do what Janie meant it to do now. She looked around again. She habitually sat in the back of class; it was easier to read books behind her text that way, but it was still hard to be inconspicuous with a piece of wood over a foot long. She rubbed the surface of her desk with her sleeve to clean it. A mirror would have been ideal, but any reflective surface would do. Then, when Mr. Lambert turned his back to demonstrate an equation on the board, she pulled out the rowan wand and rapidly drew a near-perfect circle on the desk, leaving only a tiny break in the line near the top.

By now the girls on either side were regarding her as if she had gone mad. Janie cupped her arms protectively around the circle and gave them a killing look. When they turned away she placed her left thumb precisely to bridge the gap in the circle, clasped the rowan stick with her right hand, breathed directly on the center, and murmured four short words.

Instantly she felt a tremendous rush of heat. The line she had inscribed flared translucent red, as if she had opened a very thin window onto fire. There was a puff of heat against her face and the center of the desk seemed to drop out. Janie stared, appalled. A visioning circle was not supposed to be like this. Instead of being crystal clear and silvery, this circle was murkily red, shot through with cadaverous cracks of green. Shapes moved blurrily, sluggishly, inside it, but it was impossible to make anything out. For a moment Janie wondered wildly if she'd managed to cast a circle into Hell, or Betelguese, or some other equally improbable place, and then something vaguely familiar swam into her field of vision. Two dark spots that might, with a little imagination, be turned into eyes, a paler prominence of nose between them. Below, a large black O of a mouth. Wide open—in horror, seemingly. A face. And, yes, definitely familiar. She'd done it. She'd managed to hook into Claudia.

▾ ▾ ▾

Claudia nearly bit the eraser off her pencil when the top of her desk turned red. Paralyzed, she stared into the copper-colored circle, which was full of moving things like the ghosts on a TV with very, very bad reception—or like things in certain dreams which Claudia had never told anyone about and never would. Then she slid her spelling paper farther out of the way and saw Janie's face, pale green in the strange light, and she went limp with relief.

Janie's voice came out of the desk, quite faint, and sounding as if she were speaking underwater. "Claudia! Claudia, is that you?"

Claudia cast a hunted look around. "Yes," she whispered, hunching close to the apparition. She wondered if anyone else could see it.

"Did you send me a letter?"

From the front of the room, Mrs. Anderson glanced up. Claudia's stomach lurched. "Yes," she whispered, even more softly, almost touching the desk with her lips.

"Well, what did it *say?*"

Claudia felt a little wave of sadness—though not surprise—that Janie hadn't been able to read her letter. "It said, 'earthquake,' " she whispered in agony, mouth near Janie's image, eyes on Mrs. Anderson. "The birds say— 'earthquake.' And all the cans will fall on Remmy Garcia . . ." Mrs. Anderson stood abruptly, and Claudia panicked. She wasn't at all sure which would be worse, having the cans fall on Remmy Garcia or having Mrs. Anderson see Janie in her desk. It was a fine point, and too much for Claudia to contend with in her present state of mind. She seized her spelling paper and dragged it back over Janie's face.

Janie's voice came even more faintly, but demandingly. "Claudia! I'm losing you! Claudia, I need to know *when.* When is there going to be an earthquake?"

Mrs. Anderson was walking down the aisle. Claudia glanced at Remmy Garcia's brown head, gulped, and made the ultimate sacrifice. She lifted the bottom of the spelling paper and hissed underneath it:

"I don't know! They don't know, either! They just say soon! Oh, Janie, help us, help us!"

Then she slapped the paper back down, banged her clasped hands hard on top of it, and raised a terrified face to her teacher.

▾ ▾ ▾

Janie felt the circle tremble and begin to break away from her. She exhaled sharply and let it go. When her vision cleared she saw the students around her gathering books and backpacks, heading for the door. Several of them lingered to give her odd glances: had she been summoning demons or just having an epileptic fit? She ignored them. After a few minutes of quiet breathing, she slipped the wand into her backpack and left.

If asked, Janie Hodges-Bradley probably would have agreed with Bliss Bascomb's evaluation of her appearance. It was generally acknowledged that Janie's brother Charles, with his fair hair and blue-gray eyes, had inherited all the good looks in the family. Alys, the eldest, shared the same coloring, and though not exactly pretty, she seemed to radiate good health and energy.

Janie looked like none of the others, and least of all like Charles, her twin. There was no conventional beauty about her, but there was something arresting in her tangled black hair and her pale skin. And her eyes were neither blue nor gray but simply purple. Most people stopped to look at her twice.

Just now there was a stinging in those purple eyes. Marvelous. She'd probably burst a blood vessel, straining that way. And for what? All very well for Claudia to say "help us," but what on earth could Janie do? Janie was no sorceress, no wielder of even a lowly Green or Brown Staff. She was not even a proper apprentice, being human and not one of the Finderlais, the Wildfolk.

But . . . she had managed to cast a visioning circle, after only a year and a half of training—and with a rowan wand, no less. And she might be a human, but she was a smart human. Alys would never forgive her if she didn't at least try to help.

Bliss Bascomb was at the end of the hallway, with two other girls. They stopped talking as Janie went by only to resume in whispers when she was past. Janie willed herself to keep on walking, but her hand clenched almost involuntarily on the rowan stick inside her backpack.

Just once, oh, just once. If that stupid, simpering Bliss only knew what might happen. But Janie remembered quite well the time she had mentioned it to Morgana. She had asked the sorceress if there were such a thing as a spell to discomfort your enemy, and Morgana had given her a quick, level look out of those strange gray eyes of hers and said, "Of course." And with one sharp movement she'd opened a book and tossed to Janie a faded piece of parchment. Janie, reading it, had stiffened.

"But, Morgana," she'd said, after a minute. "This—is a killing spell."

"Of course," Morgana had said, in exactly the same tone as before, and still watching her. "A sorceress does not *discomfort* her enemies. If they are important enough to deal with by sorcery, they are important enough to kill. You cannot turn the Wild Arts to trifles. Do you wish to learn the spell?"

Janie had held her gaze a moment, then looked away, yielding. "No." Before Morgana could say anything else she'd added grimly, "I get the point."

So, now, walking away from Bliss, feeling the stiffness in her shoulders and the flush in her face, Janie made herself think about other things. About Claudia, who was in trouble.

The sight of the public phone in the amphitheater gave her an idea. Morgana did, in fact, have a telephone, though she very seldom used it.

But the line rang and rang with no answer. Which was hardly surprising. The sorceress could be anywhere, down in her secret workroom or out in the wilderness of gardens behind the old house, and she would never hear it.

Well, that was that. Janie had done all that a reasonable person could do. But she somehow felt, as she tapped the earpiece of the phone absently against her lips, that this would not satisfy Alys. Alys, if she were here, would demand that Janie do something *unreasonable,* but also something that worked. And then there was Claudia, in third grade, with cans of some sort about to fall on her head.

Right, then. Well, what would Alys do?

The tapping slowed. Janie's eyes, fixed on the telephone buttons, narrowed, then creased at the corners. She tried, and failed, to repress a smile.

Well, now, why not? It was certainly unreasonable enough.

As the bell for her next class rang she began to punch in the telephone number of Serrano Elementary School. She was grinning and her eyes were glowing violet.

▾ ▾ ▾

Claudia shuffled her feet uneasily. Cautiously, she chanced leaning out of line to look past other silent, fidgeting children at Mrs. Anderson, who was huddled with two other teachers on the blacktop.

They had been standing there for half an hour. The whole school. Claudia had no idea how Janie had managed it, but not five minutes after she had slammed the spelling paper over her sister's face, while Mrs. Anderson was still in the middle of a lecture about Claudia and Claudia's grades and Claudia's attitude, the bells had begun to sound. *Not* the duck-and-cover, but the fire drill. All the children had filed out to the field, where they had been standing ever since. Claudia's fear, now, was that they would be released and sent back to class before the quake came.

Even as she thought it, even as someone behind her said, "Hey, what are the *police*—" she swayed a little on her feet.

No, it was the ground swaying—everyone had felt it. The birds were in a frenzy. All other sound had stopped. Claudia saw the line of children break up as some stumbled to the right and some to the left. Everything began to shake hard. Children were crying, holding on to each other. Belatedly, far away in the empty school, the bells began to sound the duck-and-cover.

▼ ▼ ▼

In American History 1B, Charles Hodges-Bradley raised his chin from his fist and scowled at the boy next to him.

"Quit it, Talbott," he muttered.

Talbott bristled. "I wasn't. *You* quit it."

"*I* didn't do it, *you* did. Leave my desk alone."

"Back off, jerk."

"Make me, creep."

Talbott opened his mouth to frame a suitable reply, then stopped dead. Both boys stared at each other, and expressions of unholy glee broke over their faces simultaneously.

"Earthquake!" shouted Talbott to the class at large. "Hey! Earthquake! Earthquake!"

"Ladies and gentlemen," said Charles through a megaphone made of his homework paper, "we interrupt this program to announce—"

"Under the *desks,*" broke in the teacher, as bells began to shrill. "Under that desk, Hodges-Bradley! I mean it. All the way! Anything sticking out, I kick!"

"This is great," whispered Talbott, grinning amicably from under his own desk. "Isn't this great?"

Charles nodded. The back-and-forth sensation was certainly interesting to start with. It was just that it kept going.

It was okay with him if it stopped now. Yes, it really was okay if it stopped. . . .

▾   ▾   ▾

Alys Hodges-Bradley was in the outfield, running, reaching for a high fly ball, when something picked the ground up and shook it once, hard. The ball smacked down, unheeded, at a little distance, as Alys turned and stared. All action in the softball game was suspended. Something shook the ground again, and kept shaking it. Sirens and school bells broke the unearthly silence.

Alys took two steps on the suddenly unstable ground, then stopped. There was nothing she could do. Claudia and Charles and Janie were far away. By the time she reached them it would all be over.

Someone was pointing at the high-school pool, where the water sloshed back and forth, spilling out first at one side, then the other. Alys could keep her balance on the rolling ground if she tried, but her legs didn't want to. They folded quietly under her and she sat under the hot bright sun, clenching grass tightly between her fingers, willing the world to be still.

▾   ▾   ▾

Janie Hodges-Bradley wedged herself more firmly in the doorway of the girls' rest room and glared at a lowly seventh grader who had also found refuge there. She didn't like thrill rides and she was beginning to feel seasick. Enough was enough.

▾ ▾ ▾

THREE

In Fell Andred

When the world settled into place again Claudia let go of Susan Parlin and cautiously raised her head. Teachers were standing up, moving around, comforting students. Kids were sobbing. Claudia stayed with her class as parents, first by ones and twos and then in a flood, came to pick up their children. A man with a megaphone tried to keep order, telling all the remaining students to stay until someone came for them. But in the shadows near the school building Claudia had glimpsed a lithe red shape. She slipped quietly away and in a moment the vixen was in her arms, wet nose on her neck and jaw.

"Yes, yes, indeed, to be certain," said the vixen, wriggling as Claudia hugged her tightly, breathing in the dusty half-wild smell. "That is to say, yes, but not here in public. Have you broken any bones? No? Then stop sniveling and come along. Morgana wants you."

They detoured to pick up a grimy Charles and a scowling Janie along the way. Alys was not to be found.

▾ ▾ ▾

Alys was the last to reach Morgana's house that afternoon, for the simple reason that she had gone first to the junior high and then to the elementary school, and finally home, before realizing where the others must be. As she walked her bike up the long gravel driveway under the tall, shading eucalyptus trees, she felt again the sense of isolation the old house always gave her. Fell Andred was very much a place apart, a place that existed beside, but did not quite belong to, the rest of the world.

She went around to the back of the square gray mansion, passing the front doors that had not been opened in a hundred years. She did not knock, but let herself in, and then stood listening to the silence.

"Hello?" she said. "Morgana? Janie?"

The great room, which had once been a dining hall, but which Morgana used as a living room, was empty. So was the spacious, oak-beamed kitchen. Uncomfortable, Alys hesitated, not liking to shout. Fell Andred was so large and echoing, and had such an air of quietly waiting and watching that it always dampened her spirits. It would be like shouting in a church.

She sighed in worry and frustration. She would have to search for them. But they could be in any of the dozens of strangely shaped, oddly furnished rooms or outside somewhere on the vast grounds. It could take hours.

She turned first to the little stairway off the kitchen, which led straight down into the cellar. It was cool and dark as always. At the far end of the cellar was an apparently solid wall. Squinting, Alys approached it, located the faint outlines of a door in the boards, and slipped her fingers into a knothole. She paused a moment, feeling the spring mechanism under her fingertips. No one ever disturbed Morgana Shee at her work. But Alys was annoyed and anxious and didn't really believe Morgana was inside.

She pressed the spring hard, heard the click, and felt the door swing away.

"Oh—oh, excuse me—I'm so sorry—"

She had a glimpse of Morgana's startled face, and of another face, unnaturally colored and apparently floating in air above a device of twisted copper wires on the worktable. In the briefest of instants Alys felt there was something familiar about that face, and then a green hum flashed past her cheek, circled her head once, and whizzed off into the cellar.

"Darion Beldar!" cried the sorceress, slamming a fist on the table. Whether it was a curse or a plea for assistance Alys didn't know. Thrusting Alys aside the sorceress pursued the green hum.

"I'm sorry—I'm so sorry—"

Sorceress and quarry had both shot up the stairs. Alys turned back in dismay to look at the workroom. The face above the twisted wires had vanished; the wires themselves were smoking. Evidence of the recent earthquake was every-where: bottles smashed on the floor, retorts overturned, shelves in disarray. The Gold Staff lay on the worktable, looking, as it always did when not in Morgana's hands, exactly like an old brass fire iron. Alys gave it a wide berth. Beneath one shelf was a drawer that she had never noticed before; it seemed to have popped out of the wall. As she waited uneasily for Morgana's return her eyes fell on what lay inside.

A sword, a beautiful sword. There were other instruments that she did not recognize, but from the first it was the sword that held her attention. Long and straight and clean, with pure singing lines, very plain, and very, very beautiful. She had reached out to touch it before she knew what she was doing. Her hand clasped the hilt, and it felt *wonderful* there, just right, and then she gasped and let go. It had *burned* her. Or—no—it had been more like an electric shock searing through her hand and up her arm to the shoulder. An agonizing, aversive sensation, like the feeling when you barely save yourself from falling and the adrenalin rushes through you . . .

Wounded, rubbing her arm and shaking her hand alternately, Alys realized that somehow, incredibly, she was almost tempted to pick it up again.

While she stood indecisively she heard a step.

The returning sorceress was not pleased. Her clear gray eyes pinned Alys briefly to the wall, and then moved around the room to rest on the smoking wires.

"Did you touch anything?"

"I—no," said Alys, utterly shocked at herself.

"Never touch anything in here." There was something green between Morgana's cupped palms; she opened them above the wires and the green flowed out into the device. It stopped smoking and flared brightly; now a featureless copper-colored sphere. Morgana placed it in the drawer and the drawer slid back into the wall, perfectly concealed.

"I'll go away," said Alys humbly.

"And high time." Once more the odd gray eyes fixed on her and Alys realized she was still rubbing her elbow. She stopped, feeling guilty. "Your brother and sisters are above," said Morgana slowly, still watching her.

Alys started. She had forgotten all about them. Remorsefully, wondering what she had interrupted and why Morgana was doing it practically in the middle of an earthquake, she turned and went back up the stairs.

Seeing the others revived her. "Is everybody all right?"

"Sure," said Charles. "Want a cookie?"

Claudia was sitting at the kitchen table with the vixen in her arms, stroking the familiar's red-gold fur. The vixen was bearing this passively. Alys hugged her smaller sister, examined her for bruises, and absently licked a finger to wipe a smudge from her face, all the while saying:

"Well, you could have left a note or something, couldn't you? I've been looking for you everywhere."

Janie, glancing up through spiky lashes at the doorway behind Alys, murmured, "But you aren't supposed to go *everywhere*—are you?"

"We were out at the henhouse," Charles put in hastily, as Alys gathered herself for a reply to this. The hens were Claudia's, but she kept them at Morgana's house because their mother said that one rabbit and any number of stray cats in their own backyard was enough.

"No bickering, please," added the vixen, her sleepy eyes as gold as the collar around her neck. So Alys turned back to Claudia, who had been trying to get her attention.

"I'm all right because of Janie," she was saying, looking up seriously at Alys. "She saved us. Me and Remmy Garcia and everybody. I looked in the room afterward and the cans were all over and there were dents in the desks. Most of the cans were dented, too. I guess we won't win the food drive now," Claudia finished sadly, as if this thought had just occurred to her.

"Dents in the desks? Food drive?" Alys looked at Janie in alarm.

Janie shrugged. "Apparently they had an earthquake hazard in the kiddies' classroom. Claudia knew what was going to happen and sent a note to me. So I arranged to get them all out of the building before the quake hit. That's all. It was nothing much."

Alys ignored this patent fishing for compliments. "How?" she demanded.

Janie grinned. "I called in a bomb threat. They evacuated the whole school out onto the blacktop. According to Claudia the police are still swarming all over."

"You did *what?*" said Alys, scandalized.

Janie's grin disappeared and her jaw thrust out. "Listen, if you think you could have done a better job—"

Morgana's voice broke in.

"I should like to know how Claudia knew what was going to happen, when I did not, myself."

The sorceress had come up the stairs so softly that no one had noticed her.

"The birds—" began Claudia, and stopped.

Janie winced. Morgana had given Claudia the charm to allow her to speak to the vixen outside the old house. Within the walls of Fell Andred all true languages were the same, but the charm was supposed to enable Claudia to understand the vixen anywhere. The bit about all animals had been Janie's idea, and she had quietly incised one extra line on the bloodstone when Morgana wasn't looking. Somewhat to her surprise it had worked.

"The birds?" repeated Morgana, settling into utter stillness. Then she swiftly crossed the room and lifted the amulet on its chain out of Claudia's shirt. She studied it for a moment, front and back, and her eyebrows went up.

"Janie," she said, over her shoulder, without looking at that young lady.

"Uh . . . yes, madam?"

"We'll discuss this later."

Janie wilted. "Yes, madam."

Morgana weighed the amulet in her hand, started to lift it off Claudia's neck. She stopped. Claudia was gazing up at her, mouth slightly open, distress and naked pleading in her eyes. The sorceress shook her head slightly, sighed, and tucked the charm back inside Claudia's shirt.

Alys, meanwhile, was feeling ashamed. She made an effort. "I'm sorry, Janie," she said. "I guess I'm still a little upset. You were right to get them out of school."

"What're you so upset about?" said Charles cheerfully. "It was only an earthquake."

"Yes," said Alys, under her breath, "but *was* it only an earthquake?" She raised her eyes to Morgana. "On the radio at home they're saying that there've been quakes all up and down the line of the San Andreas fault. No real damage anywhere, but tremors all the way up to San Francisco. Nothing like it has ever happened before—the seismologists can't explain it."

"I daresay they can't. But, of course, they're looking at it from the wrong point of view. Not 'all along the line of the fault'—all along the line of the Passage."

"The Passage to the Wildworld?" cried Charles. "You mean it's coming open?"

"Not beneath your feet," said Morgana dryly. "But you must realize that the Western Passage was not always confined to the mirrors in this house. Originally, it ran all the way up the coast to the Wildworld city of Weerien, the seat of the Weerul Council—in the same area as San Francisco is in this world. When the Council decreed that all the Passages between the worlds be closed I realized I would have to find some way to shorten it, to concentrate its power, if I wanted to keep it open. Those were the Council's terms: I could remain here in my husband's world if I could tame the Passage enough to guarantee that no one but I myself could use it."

"So you made the mirrors . . ." said Alys softly. "But now that they're broken—"

"If you remember, I broke the mirrors and closed the Passage on the night of the solstice itself, with the moon still rising in the sky. The resistance was terrible."

Alys shivered. It had been a year and a half, but the details of that night, the night she and Charles and Janie and Claudia had helped turn back an army of invading sorcerei, were burned into her memory forever. They very nearly hadn't been able to do it, very nearly hadn't found Morgana to free her from Cadal Forge's spell. If not for Janie, who had finally thought to look in the least likely place of all, Cadal Forge would have won. Cadal Forge the master sorcerer, the Red Staff wielder, the madman who hated all humans, would have won.

Morgana's voice drew Alys's attention back to the present.

"And now, although the mirrors are broken forever, and there is no chance of the Passage reopening here, I fear that farther north it may be unstable. Especially if—someone—is trying to force it open."

"Someone?" Alys said. The chill she felt this time was deeper. Cadal Forge had been formidable in his madness, almost invincible, but there was someone worse, someone who was trusted throughout the Wildworld, who sat on the Council itself, who would never be suspected of treachery. Someone utterly sane and utterly ruthless and right this minute free in the human world.

She made her voice work, flatly. "Thia Pendriel."

Everyone in the kitchen had gone quiet; even Janie's purple eyes were grim. Alys would have bet that they were all picturing the tall councillor, remembering her sweet persuasive voice and her deep red hair and her staff of twisted silver. She was almost a felt presence among them.

"Thia Pendriel," agreed Morgana, her voice equally flat. "Who else? She now has not only her staff but also the Gem she has stolen. With those together there is little beyond her power."

"It's just that it's been so long . . . and we didn't hear anything about her. . . . I thought that maybe—"

"She had died or departed? No. A sorceress of her stature is not killed easily. And where would she go except back to Findahl? But for that she needs a Passage."

Of all the sorcerei only Thia Pendriel, Silver Guildmistress and Morgana's age-old enemy, had escaped being forced back into the Wildworld when they had shut the mirrors. She had disappeared into the dark and silence outside Fell Andred. But first she had stolen the Gem of Power which Cadal Forge had brought to wreak his vengeance on the human world, she had stolen Heart of Valor. A fistful of red ice, an uncut ruby the size of a plum. One of the Forgotten Gems. With it, she had power almost beyond imagination.

"But, *why?*" Alys burst out, frustrated. "Why does she want to go back now, Morgana? Why did she even come here in the first place? She could have taken the Gem from Cadal Forge any time in the Wildworld. Why come all the way into the human world only to get trapped and then leave without accomplishing anything?"

"I have thought on that," said Morgana. "And in these last few days I fear I have found the answer. You are wrong to say she has accomplished nothing, Alys. Just this last week she has done something I would not have thought possible. And there is more she means to do . . . if she is not stopped.

"And that, children," said Morgana, straightening and looking at all of them levelly, "is why I have sent for you today. To bid you good-bye. I must go north, must stop her—if it can be done."

"You're leaving?"

"Tonight. If I am right there is little time left, a few days at most."

"But what is it she's doing? What do you have to stop?"

Morgana glanced at Janie, then, slowly, turned back to Alys. "I think," she said, "that it is best if you do not know that. Even as it is, I am not happy about leaving you here. Things are astir. There are—but never mind. You have your parents' protection, and you will have the vixen. You will not be alone."

The vixen had struggled out of Claudia's arms to sit on the table when Morgana appeared. Now the fur on her back lifted.

"What do you mean 'they will have the vixen'?" she said suspiciously.

"I leave you in charge," said Morgana, still addressing Alys. Janie raised her eyebrows but said nothing. "Try not to do anything foolish. I will give Janie a way of summoning me back, in case of direst need. But that means a matter of life or death, do you understand?"

"Yes," said Alys.

"What do you mean, 'they will have the vixen'?" said the vixen, louder.

"You should have no reason to use it. Any ill to come should come in the north."

"What do you mean, 'they will have the vixen'?"

"I should think that would be plain enough!" snapped Morgana, rounding on her. "I mean that I am leaving you here."

"I will not be left."

"You will do as I say, and you will stop arguing about it."

The vixen's eyes were narrow slits of gold. Her tail was bristling.

"You may need my help—"

"I'll have to manage without it."

"By the bond we share—"

"By the bond you wear! You have no choice but to obey me."

The vixen seemed to flinch under the golden collar, but she tried again. "I won't have you going off alone," she grumbled.

"How many times must I say it? You are my familiar, not the head of my Guild! You are bound to my service *and you will do as I say.*"

There was a long silence while the vixen and the sorceress fought it out, eye to eye. Then, in a sudden fluid motion, the vixen leaped off the table and was out of the kitchen. Alys cringed in embarrassment.

Morgana let out her breath.

"You will have the vixen," she repeated, not looking at anyone. "And your parents. You will not be alone."

Alys glanced at the others. Charles was looking at her. Claudia was fingering the amulet, her face closed and tense, like someone watching her parents have a fight. Janie was expressionless.

"Sure," Alys said hollowly. "We'll be fine."

Morgana let out another breath, almost like a sigh. Usually, despite her diminutive stature, the sorceress seemed fearfully and thoroughly adult. But just now to Alys she appeared more like a young girl, a girl with a cloud of dark hair and a pale, drawn face.

"We'll be fine," said Alys again, more convincingly. On impulse, she laid her hand on Morgana's arm—and flinched. A tingling had shot down her arm through her hand, leaping to Morgana. Morgana also flinched, and the young girl was gone. The sorceress looked at Alys sharply and frowned.

"North," Charles was musing, unaware of this byplay. "North, eh? I don't suppose you'll run into Elwyn."

"What?" said Morgana, distracted, turning the frown on him.

"Uh, Elwyn," said Charles, rubbing his forehead and looking very casual. "You know, when she left, she said she was going north. She said she wanted to visit Holly's Wood."

"And? So?"

"Well, if you do run into her . . . well, I just thought—you could . . . uh . . . say 'hi.' "

The greatest sorceress since Darion the Nightweaver looked down at him for a long moment in silence. Charles withered.

"I think," she said at last, "that you would be well advised to forget my half sister. I doubt very much if she remembers *you*. And if she does—" Morgana suddenly leaned forward and brushed the hair off Charles's face. "Hmmf!" she said uncommunicatively, staring at him.

Charles was red and choking. "I didn't mean—I don't care—"

"As well you don't. Janie, I will need to do some study before I go. Come, please." She headed for the library.

Still sputtering, Charles gathered himself up with affronted dignity. "I—I—well, what are you two looking at? And—and anyway, why didn't you tell her?" he said, turning on Alys.

"Tell her what? *Oh!* That. I suppose," said Alys slowly, "because I was afraid if I did tell her she might feel she had to stay. And I think,"—even more slowly—"that perhaps she really needs to go."

They stayed in the kitchen until dinnertime. When they

left Alys stopped by the library door, which was ajar. She didn't dare open it, for fear of letting little green things out. About to knock, she was arrested by the sound of Morgana's voice.

"—keeping a very close watch," Morgana was saying earnestly. "There are signs only a sister would note. I might stay a little longer. The danger will—"

But Alys was tired of being dishonest. She could bear to eavesdrop no more. She knocked, loudly.

"I—I've just come to say that we're leaving," she said, looking around the door at Morgana's summons. "Don't stay too late, Janie."

Janie looked noncommittal.

"Good-bye, Morgana. And—good luck."

The little sorceress, wielder of a Gold Staff, smiled across the room at her. "Thank you," she said, not dryly but quite seriously. "I will need it. But all may yet be well. Watch over them, Alys."

"Uh, I'll try," said Alys. There were times when you forgot for weeks why you had ever liked Morgana, and then you suddenly were reminded, and you didn't know what to do. Alys was caught between the impulse to hug her, to curtsey, and to cry. Instead, she blurted out, "Good-bye!" and fled.

Their own house looked small and flat and ordinary after Morgana's. But at the foot of their driveway, Charles gave an exclamation and seized Alys's arm.

"Look! Did you see that?"

"What?"

"On the roof—by the chimney. A sort of black thing. Furry. There—it's gone now. I guess it was a cat."

Alys felt uneasy. "Are you sure?"

"Sure I'm sure. What else would it be?" He grinned suddenly, his usual high spirits returning. "Black beavers from Mordor?"

Alys waved this away, annoyed. But, inside, she looked up the fireplace. The flue was shut. She flipped it back and forth a few times, frowning.

"Hey, Alys," came Charles's voice from the kitchen. "Do you think we should, like, check for gas leaks or something? Because they say after an earthquake—"

"I already did," she answered, joining him. "And I checked the water heater and I left a message on the answering machine saying we were all right, in case anybody called. *That's* why I was so late."

"Good old Alys," said Charles affectionately. "You're so responsible."

Yes, good old Alys, thought Alys bleakly. Responsible old Alys, who had opened a door she was never supposed to have opened and ruined Morgana's spell. Reliable old Alys, who had touched something she shouldn't have touched. Honest old Alys, who had told two major lies today, and even now she wasn't sure which of the two was worse.

Practical old Alys, who was now going to make dinner because otherwise there wasn't going to *be* any dinner, she thought, heading Charles off at the refrigerator. There she paused, grasping the handle, her eyes on the itinerary held to the refrigerator door by a magnet. *April 24–27: Bangkok.*

The Oriental Hotel it read. *April 27–29: Chiang Mai. The Royal Orchid. April 29–May 2: Ban Chiang. Private accommodation provided* . . .

Bon voyage, Mom and Dad, she thought, missing them terribly. Then, absentmindedly rubbing her arm, she reached in to get some hamburger.

F O U R
▾   ▾   ▾

Talisman

Alys swatted at the offending alarm clock, then looked at it blearily and groaned. She felt as if she hadn't gotten ten minutes of solid sleep last night. And her arm and shoulder were stiff—she must have lain on them wrong.

She kept working them to get the kinks out as she washed and dressed. The silence downstairs gave her some misgivings, but when she reached the kitchen she found her three siblings scrubbed and shining, placidly eating breakfast. The illusion of domestic comfort was dispelled when she got a closer look.

"Not right out of the *jar*, Claudia," she said, rescuing a spoon and the strawberry preserves from her youngest sister.

Claudia wiggled helplessly, waving sticky fingers in the air as Alys applied a dishtowel to her face.

"Charles put chocolate chips in his cereal," she said darkly, emerging from the towel.

"Don't you think you're sort of overdoing the protective older sister bit?" asked Charles as Alys peered into his bowl and confiscated it. He poured chocolate chips directly from the bag into his mouth.

"The only reason Mrs. Delveccio isn't staying here right now is that I promised Mom and Dad I could make you eat properly and take a bath everyday. But, obviously—"

"Anyway, Janie didn't get in until two o'clock in the morning," said Charles quickly, eager to spread the blame over as wide an area as possible.

"What? Janie, is that true?"

Janie continued to spoon cereal calmly into her mouth without looking up from the book she had propped open before her. "Yes."

"Why? What were you doing?"

"Putting up wards around this house and Morgana's, among other things."

"If Mom and Dad were here you wouldn't dare, Janie. From now on you get in at a decent hour. Understand?"

Janie didn't answer directly. Instead she gave Alys a cool and quizzical look. "What's the matter with your arm?"

Alys stopped kneading her shoulder. "Nothing's the matter with my arm!" she almost shouted. After a moment she sighed and bowed her head. "Sorry."

Charles and Claudia had taken advantage of her distraction to make their escape with the chocolate chips. Heaving another sigh, Alys began to clear the table.

"How do the wards work?" She spoke without looking at Janie, as she stacked bowls in the sink.

"They're like a—security system. They surround the entire house; two layers in a sort of octagon shape with one central anchor above. That way nothing can get in from outside unless we let it. They'll also warn me automatically if something nasty gets too near."

"Janie. What is Morgana so afraid of?"

There was a pause. "It's quite normal for a sorceress to

set wards around her house when she has to leave. . . ."

Alys turned around and looked at her.

"All right, you're right. She is afraid. But I don't know why! That's the truth, Alys. She didn't tell me.

"She did say one thing," Janie added. "At the time of the earthquake the Passage opened, just for an instant. And Morgana sensed that something—or things—came through from the Wildworld. Of course, they might not be harmful things, but when you're dealing with the Wildfolk it's better to be safe."

"If it was just open for an instant—"

"Alys, the Passage is over five hundred miles long. It runs almost exactly along the line of the San Andreas fault. It's there because that's where two pieces of the earth's crust come together—and please don't ask me why until you've studied plate tectonics! And with all that length opening up, even just for an instant, it's hardly surprising that something somewhere got through."

"But not around here, surely. Morgana said the one place the Passage was shut tight was right here."

"Magic is drawn to magic. And right now there are only three hot spots of magic in California: Morgana, wherever she is, and Thia Pendriel, wherever she is, and *us!*"

Alys digested this moodily. "I suppose there's no chance Thia Pendriel went back to the Wildworld when the Passage opened for an instant?"

"Morgana says she did not. Morgana says"—Janie looked down at her clasped hands soberly—"that she will wait until Beltane. That's May first—Sunday. There's something else

Thia Pendriel has to do before she can leave, and Beltane is the best time to do it. And don't ask what it is, because Morgana didn't tell me!"

"All right, but I just hate not knowing what's going on. And that reminds me, when I, uh, walked in on Morgana downstairs yesterday, she was doing some hocus-pocus with a green thing that flew. What was it?"

Janie looked severe. "It was a visioning sphere—like a visioning circle only much more powerful—and you're not even supposed to know such things exist, much less see them! Any other questions?"

"Yes." Alys was tempted to ask Janie what Morgana had been talking about in the library, when she had warned Janie about watching for signs only a sister would note. But she couldn't quite bring herself to do it. Instead she asked, "So, what's the bracelet?"

Janie touched the thick copper band on her wrist. It looked ancient and heavy, like something found in an Egyptian tomb, and had a single white crystal set in the center. "This is the means Morgana left of summoning her if anything terrible happens. She has a bracelet just like it. If I break my crystal her crystal shatters, too."

Alys gazed down at the bracelet in silence, trying not to picture what would have to happen before they were entitled to use it.

Janie saw her face. "I know," she said softly. "But whatever it is Morgana is afraid of, we're well protected. The wards are *strong*. And"—she settled back and spoke very briskly all at once—"I might as well tell you that I've thought of a way to make them stronger, and I'm going to do it today. I'm going to get myself a familiar."

A disembodied voice came from the hallway. "I hear they have an iguana for sale over at ProPets."

Janie and Alys both turned to see Charles and Claudia shamelessly eavesdropping. Alys tried to look stern.

"You might as well come back in."

"You don't buy a familiar," Janie added coldly. "You trap it and bargain with it. Or rescue it and gentle it, like Morgana did with the vixen. And then it helps you do magic, like strengthening the wards. Every proper sorceress has a familiar, and it's high time I did, too."

Alys wondered why Janie had waited for Morgana's departure to decide it was high time, but all she said was, "How?"

Janie and Claudia exchanged a complicit glance. "There is a fox," said Janie, deliberately, "down at Irvine Park. In a cage. I'm going down there tonight to let it out."

"You most certainly are not!" Alys's first impulse was to quash this idea of Janie's entirely. And yet, what harm could come to Janie in the park? They had played there all their lives. And if it were true that another familiar would strengthen the protective wards it was surely a good cause.

There was another reason for yielding, which Alys would scarcely admit even to herself. In her secret heart she was not sure that she could stop Janie if she tried. In most matters Janie was cautious and prudent almost to a fault—but not in magic. There was something about sorcery that got her blood up. She took mad chances and seemed quite detached about the consequences, as if it were all part of some hypothetical experiment she were conducting. It worried Alys.

"At least," she said, coming to a decision, "you're not going alone."

"No; I figured you would want to come. I want you. And I want Claudia, too, to talk to the fox. I don't particularly care whether Charles comes or not," Janie added candidly.

"What? Leave my three helpless sisters running around in the dark by themselves? Never! Charles is coming, all right! Say," he added thoughtfully, "you don't suppose they've canceled school today? Because of the earthquake?"

"School's open," said Janie. "It was on the radio."

"In that case, how about calling in another bomb threat? At the junior high. I could dial for you—"

"None of us is going anywhere tonight," said Alys to Janie, ignoring him, "unless the vixen agrees it's okay."

▾　▾　▾

The vixen, surprisingly, had no objections.

"I'll come, myself," she said, when they had gathered in the old house after school to ask her. "It will be something useful to do, anyway. Left behind like this to baby-sit! The only trouble you four are likely to get into is that which you make for yourselves." She got quite worked up about it, and all Claudia's soothings could not calm her. But she agreed to meet them after dark.

▾　▾　▾

Alys usually found some time everyday to spend with her horse; today she simply went a little later and waited for the others to join her. She leaned her forehead dreamily against Winter's warm neck as she brushed him with the currycomb, remembering what Morgana had said when she had first given him to her as a colt.

"A small token of my appreciation," the sorceress had said, and had added, "Every hero needs a horse."

Charles had snorted, "But Alys isn't a hero."

And Morgana had replied—what? At the time, Alys had been so enraptured by the idea of having a horse for her very own that she had hardly noticed. Something, she thought, about "And the colt isn't a horse . . . yet . . ."

Well, the long-legged, skittish colt had grown into a magnificent white stallion: sleek, superbly muscled, with a small, exquisite head. The hero, however, was a different matter. Alys sighed and pressed harder into Winter, sniffing up the comforting smell of clean horse. She felt no more like a hero than she had last year. If anything, she felt *less* . . .

She raised her head at the sound of the others' voices as they entered the stable, arguing.

"We can't all ride one horse," Charles was saying. "Some of us will have to walk. But if you let me take my bike . . ."

Alys tried to imagine something less inconspicuous than Charles riding his dirt bike up the river bed.

"We'll borrow Chestnut," she said, tilting her head toward the next stall, where a bay mare regarded her placidly.

By the time they started off dusk had fallen. They headed east in the blue twilight.

At the embankment of the river bed there was a movement in the pampas grass and the vixen joined them.

"She says it's a little muddy down there," Claudia reported.

The mud softened the noise of the horses' hooves. Overhead, the first stars came out.

When they reached the fence that marked the perimeter of the park, they dismounted. Alys tied the horses to the fence while Charles, sweating, went to work with the wire cutters he had brought in his backpack. When he had cut three sides of a rectangle in the fence he pulled it open like a door.

"After you, Alphonse."

It was dark enough now that they needed the flashlight. The river bed here was quite dry, and rocky. Janie spoke to Alys in a low voice as they walked.

"When I was here last week I asked one of the park rangers about security. She said that a truck drives around patroling once an hour."

"That's all?"

"She said anybody crazy enough to come out here after dark, what with the rattlesnakes and coyotes and bobcats and all, was welcome to it. I *think* she was joking."

Alys and Charles, who had stopped dead, now started again. They did not seem entirely reassured.

"Claudia, walk closer to me," said Alys.

"Of course she was joking," said Charles. "There's nothing out here to hurt us—"

He broke off, choking, as a scream rose from the darkness. It was unearthly, inhuman, yet it seemed to form words. The flashlight joggled wildly as everyone moved at once; Alys and Charles both trying to grab Claudia, and both trying to run. At last Alys realized that Janie was holding onto all of them, shaking with laughter.

"It's a peacock," she gasped weakly, when Alys ceased to struggle. "They keep them in the zoo area. It means we must be getting close."

Chagrined, Alys and Charles straightened their clothes and went on. The vixen, who was scouting ahead, returned and led them through wild mustard and elderberry shrubs up the embankment.

The animal compound was small; a double fence enclosing a deer habitat and some two dozen cages smelling of manure and alfalfa. Claudia was slight enough to slip through the iron bars of the first fence, but the others had to climb. Charles dealt with the second, a chain-link fence, with the air of a professional.

Squirrels chattered in one cage as the flashlight beam slid over it. Birds fluttered, in a confusion of wings, in another. The beam revealed the vixen sitting in front of the last cage, very upright, almost prim.

The fox inside was crouched at the back of the cage, watching them unwaveringly with eyes that shone orange in the light. It was bigger than the vixen, with a grizzled back and a breast the exact color of poppies.

Janie knelt. Claudia, peering in with her mouth slightly open, stood behind her.

"All right," said Janie in a slightly strained voice. "Tell him why we're here."

Alys understood every word of Claudia's explanation. She

did not understand a single word of the fox's reply, but Claudia obviously did. She was nodding.

"He says," she translated rapidly to Janie, "that his name is Talisman. He says it's seven seasons he's been here—that's almost two years, I think. He says it's dead things they feed him. He says he's hating it."

The vixen's teeth snapped together. "Stillworlder arrogance!" she spat. "To lock up an animal and feed it carrion! Animals are meant to be free, to hunt! Not to be enslaved, to wear collars, to labor over enchantments!"

Claudia translated this. Alys thought, with alarm, that it was not Stillworlders—humans—who would put a collar on a fox and make it work at enchantments, but she said nothing.

"But what does he say about being my familiar if I let him out?" persisted Janie. "Does he agree?"

"He says," chanted Claudia in a slightly sing-song voice, "that there's nothing would please him better. He says the highest ambition of any fox is to be a magic worker. He says his great-great-great-great—I can't say how many greats—grandfather was indentured to a sorcerer, in a land beyond the sea. He says that's how he got his name. I don't think he's telling the truth about that, though," she added in her own voice. "I think he's trying to impress you."

Janie's purple eyes were fixed on the orange eyes of the fox. She let out her breath.

"All right, then," she said softly. "It's a bargain."

From her own backpack she took out the rowan wand and a packet of leaves. Inside the leaves were two large seeds which she pushed into the keyhole of the padlock on the

44

cage. She blew on the padlock, applied the virtue wand, and murmured something Alys did not catch. There was a spurt of violet dust and the padlock quietly fell open.

"He says, 'wondrous,' " said Claudia.

With fitting solemnity, Janie opened the door and held out both hands. The fox bounded to meet her; then, so fast that no one really saw it happen, it bit her thumb deeply and leaped from her arms. It was a flash of silver-gray beneath white alder trees while Alys was still gaping.

The vixen's reflexes were faster. She streaked after him, and Alys, collecting her wits, followed. She plunged through the door in the first fence, tearing her sleeve, but the bars of the second fence brought her up short. The vixen might have a chance now; she did not. After another minute of staring through the bars into darkness she walked back slowly to the others.

Janie almost never cried, but she was weeping now with sheer rage and pain. Claudia was crying in sympathy. Charles, caught between his two soggy sisters, was looking rather desperate and trying unsuccessfully to rip a swath out of his T-shirt for a bandage.

"Here," he said at last, pulling the whole shirt over his head. Alys wrapped Janie's hand and helped her up.

"Let's go. Let's just get *out* of here," said Janie, pulling away.

At the second fence they met the vixen.

"She says he's gone," reported Claudia, drawing her sleeve across her nose. "She says," Claudia sniffled, "that in her opinion it's just as well. She says he might be big and handsome, but he's a liar and a rogue. He would be most unsuitable and unreliable. She says she's going to stay here tonight and if she catches him she'll teach him a lesson."

Alys gave the vixen a hard look, but she was too tired to argue. It was a morose group that made its way back down into the river bed.

As they neared the perimeter fence Alys craned her head forward, sweeping the flashlight back and forth. With a stifled exclamation she broke into a run.

"Alys! Alys! What's the matter?" cried Charles and Claudia, running after her with Janie limping behind. When they reached the fence they saw for themselves.

"Well, where are they, then?" said Janie crossly, looking at Alys as if she expected her to pull the horses out of her pocket.

Charles began, "You must have tied them wrong—"

"I did not tie them wrong! They broke free. Look, they practically dragged the whole fence with them. Something must have scared them—" Alys stopped.

There was a silence.

"Right," said Alys. "Come on."

The ground here was smooth, but covered with thick, coating mud. Soon their shoes were so heavy it was hard to lift their feet. The easiest form of locomotion was a kind of ice-skating. Claudia, of course, hit a liquid patch and fell in it, facedown.

Alys wordlessly heaved her up and gave her an arm. They trudged on, Charles now in the lead with the flashlight, shivering under Alys's thin jacket. Janie brought up the rear, still limping, though Alys had no idea why, and viciously swatting off the heads of cattails with the virtue wand in her hand.

Alys had a bare instant's warning before the attack. She heard a crackle in the bushes at the bank's edge and turned sharply. Her first impression was that those yellow eyes were the vixen's, but something deeper inside her made a lightning calculation and said too big, too far apart, too high off the ground. Charles was far away with the flashlight. Alys seized the first weapon that came to hand and met the creature, swinging hard, even as it sprang.

The ground slapped her back as the creature knocked her flat. There was a hot, rangy smell in her nostrils. Sharp teeth—predator's teeth, made for tearing flesh—yawned in her face. She rolled, getting on top of it somehow, and struck again and again with the stick. She aimed for the skull and felt a satisfying reverberation in her arm as her weapon made contact.

I've—never much—cared for—cats, she thought, punctuating each word with a full-armed blow. Razor claws slashed at her leg. The one good thing about this kind of a fight was that she had no time to be frightened, no time to plan or think or worry. She simply reacted, defending against each move of the cat's as if she were playing a hot game of tennis. And waiting for an instant of advantage. She saw one and brought the stick down with all her force directly between the golden eyes. With a yowl, the bobcat twisted and ran.

Alys dropped the stick and bent double, gasping for air.

"It's okay, it's okay, it's okay," Charles was gabbling to

Claudia, who had her arms and legs wrapped around him, having climbed him like a tree. "Alys, did it get you? Are you hurt? Talk to me!"

But Janie stood frozen, her purple eyes wide with outrage. She bent, stiffly, and picked up the virtue wand.

"Don't you ever do that again," she said to Alys. She was so angry her voice was almost a whisper. "Don't you *ever*. Do you understand me? You could have broken it!"

Alys straightened partway up, still panting, and stared. "Are you crazy?" she gasped, chest heaving. "That thing was going to break my *head*."

"You never do that again. Never. Never. Understand?"

Alys clenched her teeth. This was exactly like Janie. Or at least like the old Janie, the before-magic Janie, who had hated almost everything. "Sure," she said at last, shutting her eyes as a wave of dizziness hit her, and fighting a sudden desire to burst into giggles. Hysteria, she told herself sternly, and squelched it, along with the desire to shake Janie until her teeth rattled. She ran a hand over her leg where the thing had slashed at her and then she and Charles examined it with the flashlight. The skin was not broken, but she had four neat parallel slits in her jeans. Incredibly, that was the extent of the damage.

"Thank God," said Charles, letting out his breath.

Claudia was still trembling. "Alys, I don't want to stay here anymore. Can't we go home?"

"We'd *better*," said Alys tersely. "And fast. And quiet. And *careful*."

There were no further incidents on the way back. The horses had found their way back to the stable, blown but unharmed. Alys took care of them silently, then they all went home. At the door Alys prescribed a hot bath and bed for Claudia, and when the others went in she remained outside, staring at the sky.

She stood with folded arms, gazing fixedly at one spot, as she had in her childhood when waiting stubbornly for a shooting star. Presently the door opened and Charles stepped out onto the porch behind her.

"I didn't want Claudia to hear this," he said quietly, "but I think you had better. That wasn't a bobcat."

"Of course it was."

"You didn't see it. I had the flashlight and I got a good look. It was sort of bobcat-shaped, but—well, bunchier around the shoulders. Bigger. And, Alys . . ."

"Well?"

"I think it . . . had hands."

When the door had closed Alys turned back to the night, but now her eyes were no longer on the sky. They wandered fitfully about the yard, searching.

The door opened once more.

"It's cold," said Janie, joining her. Alys shrugged.

"I just came out," Janie said, "to thank you."

Alys flinched from the sarcasm. "For what? For organizing that terrifically successful little expedition? For nearly breaking your virtue wand? For just being me?" The fights between Alys and Janie were the most spectacular in the Hodges-Bradley family. They usually took opposite sides of any debate, but tonight Alys didn't even feel like arguing. The hero had blown it again.

"For saving us from that bobcat-thing." Janie looked at

her consideringly and frowned. "Lighten up, Alys. We're all okay; that's what's important, isn't it? We all made it. Of course"—she waggled her bandaged thumb with a grimace—"I probably have rabies, but that's beside the point."

It was a minute before Alys understood, and then she lost her breath a little. Janie was making a joke.

"You know, Janie," she said, after a moment, "sometimes you impress me."

"Sometimes," said Janie matter-of-factly, "I impress myself. Now come inside."

F I V E

▼ ▼ ▼

Charles Loses His Temper

The phone call came during breakfast the next morning. Alys flapped a silencing hand at the other three and then stuck a finger in her free ear, trying to concentrate on the voice barely audible above long-distance buzz.

"Darling, we just heard about the quake. . . . It's ten o'clock at night here. . . ." A burst of static interrupted.

"We're all okay. How are you guys?" Alys shouted back, glaring at Charles who was tugging on the phone cord, asking, "Is it Mom? Can I talk to her? It's Mom, isn't it?"

Another burst of static. Then:

". . . just fine, darling. But tomorrow we're starting with the tour group into the Tanen Range. The problem is, we won't be near a phone until Sunday at the earliest. And, sweetheart, frankly, I'm a little worried. What if you should need us? After that quake . . ."

"Uh . . ." said Alys. She pulled the phone cord away from Charles and began to twist it. "Uh . . ."

"Just say the word, hon, and we won't go. Or if you like, I can arrange for you all to stay with Aunt Eleanore. I should never have left you alone with the kids."

Alys looked at "the kids." Two pairs of blue eyes and one pair of black-fringed purple looked back steadily. She took a deep breath.

"Mom, I can take care of them, honest. And it's not as if you could stop another quake from coming, or—or stop *anything*, even if you were here. So just don't worry. Nothing's going to happen between now and Sunday."

The rest of the conversation dealt with how to get Charles to wear a clean shirt every day, and whether they had hired elephants or a jeep to take them into the jungle, and how was the rabbit. Alys hung up with a now-familiar tightening in her stomach. She *thought* she had done the right thing. But all that day, even when she was supposed to be doing plane geometry at school, she kept remembering the way one pair of purple eyes had rolled when she said nothing was going to happen before Sunday. And thinking about that, she made a tentative decision.

After school Claudia rode off on her bike to find comfort with the vixen, and Janie shut herself up in her room, rebuffing Alys's attempts to speak with her. Charles went out alone and returned several hours later, favoring his right leg. He hurried by Alys and up the stairs.

Alys put down her magazine and her apple and listened suspiciously. Above, water crashed into a bathtub.

"Charles?" she said, mounting the stairs and tapping at the bathroom door. "Charles, I know you're in there. Answer me."

There was a blithe sound, as of singing in the shower.

"Charles, you unlock this door this minute! Or else!"

A pause, then a click. Slowly the door opened, revealing her brother. He was filthy and scratches covered his arms and face. He held a bottle of hydrogen peroxide.

"So all right," he said. "So me and John Divola took our

bikes out on the old river road. So I had a little accident—"

Alys restrained herself from scolding, and merely asked, as she helped him mop up blood and apply peroxide, "How did it happen?"

Charles frowned. "I . . . I don't know. Something ran across the road and I fell off trying not to hit it." He looked at Alys and shook his head. "It was—oh, this is crazy, but for some reason I thought it looked like a kid dressed up in a lizard suit. But that doesn't make any sense. Does it?"

Alys dropped her eyes a moment. Almost to herself she murmured, "I don't know, anymore." She remained that way a moment, thinking. One thing she did know was that her tentative decision was no longer tentative.

"All right," she added briskly, looking back up at Charles. "You're mostly clean. Except—here." She swabbed a washcloth across his forehead. "Hmmm." She swabbed again, using soap. "Funny. It won't come off. I guess it must be an old scar."

"What?" said Charles, pushing back his wet bangs and peering at himself in the mirror.

"Usually your hair hides it. That must be why I never noticed it before."

Charles rubbed at the pale, round mark on his forehead, his brow creased in puzzlement. He took the washcloth from Alys and scrubbed harder. The surrounding skin turned an angry red, but the mark remained undisturbed.

Brother and sister stared at the reflection. An uneasy feeling was unwinding in Alys's stomach. The mark was an odd color, almost luminous in the harsh fluorescent lighting. It reminded her of something. . . .

Charles was leaning over the sink, almost nose to nose with his reflection. His expression was exactly that of Alys's mother when she found termite holes in the patio deck, as if a suspicion too horrible to contemplate were imposing itself on his mind. All at once he reared back.

"Where's Janie?" Without waiting for an answer he strode down the hall and flung open Janie's bedroom door.

"Don't bother to knock," said Janie, frowning from her desk. "How can I help you?"

Charles pointed a rigid finger at his forehead. "This!" he rapped out. "This—thing! Tell me it's not what I think it is."

Janie looked cagey. "And what do you think it is?"

"First you tell me if you know anything about it."

Pushing back papers, Janie regarded her desk resignedly. "Maybe you'd better sit down," she said to the paperweight.

Charles clapped a palm to his forehead and fell backward rigidly onto the bed. "I knew it! I knew it!"

"Charles, calm down. Janie, what is he talking about?"

Charles popped up again like a jack-in-the-box. "I don't care how you do it. I want this thing off!"

Addressing Alys, Janie said, "In the old days I guess they would call it a fairy mark. A fairy, or an elf, or whatever, would kiss you, and it would leave an impression."

"A fairy?" Utterly bewildered, Alys pictured Charles being bussed by a tiny pixie hovering on dragonfly wings.

"Fairy is a human word. In the Wildworld they call them Quislais."

"Elwyn!"

"Yes, Elwyn!" howled Charles from the bed. "And it's

your fault for sending me to get her from the Wildworld last year. 'She likes you,' you said. 'Lure her,' you said. Well, I lured her, all right—for all the good it did us. And now look what's happened!"

Alys rubbed her own forehead, which was beginning to ache. Trust Elwyn Silverhair to do something like this. She was Morgana's half sister, a full Quislai, and as irresponsible as she was beautiful. A year and a half ago Alys had made the mistake of seeking her as an ally in their effort to save Morgana, and now it seemed they were still facing the consequences of that decision. Immortal and eternally child-like, Elwyn's chief talent was for making trouble.

"I told you she was totally out to lunch as far as reality was concerned, but you still made me do it," Charles raved on. "And I'm telling you right now, I am not going to go around with the kiss of Glinda the Good Witch on my forehead for the rest of my days. I want it off!"

"I didn't make her kiss you," Alys pointed out, helplessly. "You let her."

"I want it off!" shouted Charles, sticking to ground he was sure of.

"Charles," said Janie, "I *can't.*"

There was a silence. Charles shut his eyes and then opened them very slowly.

"Who," he said very quietly, "can?"

Janie looked at Alys, who winced. She turned back to Charles. "No one."

"*What?*" Alys sat and put an arm around his shoulders. He didn't seem to notice.

"Nobody can take it off. The High Council in Weerien

couldn't do it. I don't think they would even try. They don't mess with the Quislais on Quislai territory."

Alys herself was bewildered. "If they're all like Elwyn—"

"They're not, but that's not the point. Yes, they're all impossible and unreliable and they may seem childish to us. But we should be glad they're that way, because their power is beyond belief. *Nothing* can stand against them when they're roused. When that happens even the greatest sorcerei keep out of their way. Fortunately it doesn't happen very often."

Charles was staring, dully, into a middle distance. "I'm going to kill her."

"You can't. But listen to me, Charles." The mad-scientist look gleamed Janie's purple eyes. "It's not all bad. There are some advantages to being marked that way. Your senses will—probably already have—become sharper. Also, the creatures who recognize Quislai law will not dare harm you. That includes beasts of air and field and water, certain sprites and elementals, and other Quislais. You might actually find it rather interesting. . . ." Her voice trailed off at the look on his face. She sighed.

Charles rose and walked leadenly to the door.

"I will be," he said, "in my room." He added, in the tone of one who has nothing left to do but laugh at fate, "If anyone ever wants to enter the Emerald City, I'm your man."

Alys bit her lip and shook her head as he left.

Then she turned to Janie. "Come on."

"Where?"

"To Morgana's. Claudia's over there alone, and I don't want her to be. Also, there's something I want to pick up."

Janie opened her mouth to argue, then shut it again. There were times when even she could see it would do no good.

▾ ▾ ▾

On Fell Andred's back path Janie stopped suddenly. She held out a downy white feather silently to Alys, eyebrows raised.

Alys frowned, lips pressed tightly together, and shook her head refusing to speculate.

The vixen was in the kitchen with Claudia, curled nose-to-tail on the broad-slabbed wooden table. She did not, Alys noted, look as if she had been in a fight the night before.

"I guess she didn't catch up with Talisman after all," Alys said.

One silken ear twitched. "As a matter of fact I did, if it's any of your business," the vixen said coolly, not opening her eyes. "If you want to know, I gave him a severe tongue-lashing."

"I don't think it did much good," said Janie, amused. She twirled the white feather between her fingers in Claudia's direction. "Outside, on the porch," she said.

Claudia bolted up, shrieking. The vixen opened an eye. Alys grabbed the feather from Janie, at the same time shoving her toward the cellar door.

"You two go out and check on them," she said breathlessly over her shoulder. "I'm going down to the workroom with Janie." She added, with a hint of desperation,

"Claudia, it's in a fox's *nature* to eat chickens."

In the workroom she faced her sister's inquisitive gaze squarely and spoke to the point.

"I want the sword," she said.

Janie did not ask her what sword. She raised her eyebrows, pursed her lips, and said, "Huh."

"There's something nasty going on, and I can't do anything to protect us. I told Mom I would take care of you guys. And to do that I need a weapon."

Janie drummed her fingers on the worktable. "That's not just any weapon," she said at last.

"Magic?" Alys rubbed her arm reflexively.

"Made by Morgana herself, almost fifteen hundred years ago. Back in the days when they called her something different, though it means the same thing. All her names really just mean Morgan the fairy, I guess because her mother was Quislai."

Janie was watching her intently, as if willing her to understand something.

"*Sidhe* is just another word for *fairy.*" Janie continued. She pronounced the word *shee.* "Morgana the fairy . . ."

Alys went very still. "Morgan LeFay."

"Right."

"But—" Alys wasn't sure what this history of the sorceress had to do with the sword. "You mean she was bad? And it's bad, too?"

"Don't be too sure the storybooks are right when they say Morgan LeFay was bad. Oh, I know, they say she was always fighting against Merlin and King Arthur. But there might be more than one side to that, and sometimes books are wrong."

"All right. I believe you. And of course I trust Morgana. And that's why"—she determinedly brought the conversation back to the point—"I want the sword. Oh, maybe I would want it anyway, even if there weren't any danger. You've probably guessed I touched it. Morgana knew, I think. But, Janie, there *is* danger, and I think the sword can help."

Janie shook her head slowly. "I'm not at all sure that Morgana would give it to you."

"Morgana isn't here. Look, Janie," she added, as her sister continued to shake her head, "I'm trying to be reasonable about this. But I've made up my mind. If you won't give it to me voluntarily I'll have to use force!"

Janie grinned outright. "I invite you to try. I think you'll find you can't force that drawer open."

"Maybe not, but I can force your teeth down past your tonsils."

Janie blinked, looked slightly affronted, then chuckled. Although Alys frequently threatened violence, no one had ever known her to use it.

"All right, then," she said finally. "But it's your responsibility. And I don't know what you're going to do with it. It's a broadsword, you probably won't even be able to lift it."

But the sword once again seemed to fit itself to Alys's hand, and she lifted it easily. There was no shock. It was lighter than it looked, made of some Wildworld metal. Two-handedly, she raised it in salute, and then suddenly she

found herself moving. *Hanging guard, moulinet, riposte*
. . . these were words she would learn only later, but the
movements were as easy and natural as breathing. She finished up in the same position she had started, in salute, then
lowered the sword.

Janie was staring at her. "Where did you learn that?"

"I didn't," said Alys. "What is this, please? This writing
on the blade?"

"Huh? Oh. That's its name. Caliborn." She was still
looking at Alys doubtfully.

"Caliborn." Alys balanced the sword in her hand and
nodded. "All right, Janie. Thanks. Now let's go see if
Claudia is missing any chickens."

Alys felt Janie's eyes on her as they went back up, and
knew that her sister had misgivings. But she herself did not
feel anxious or alarmed. In fact, she felt relaxed for the first
time in days.

▾   ▾   ▾

Alys Has a Dream

Alys still felt physically relaxed that night, but it was difficult to get to sleep. She kept thinking about the vixen, pacing and raving in front of the henhouse, and Claudia wringing her hands over the two vanished chickens. They had returned from Morgana's house under rapidly clouding skies.

She shifted position, leaning over the bed to check on the sword, which lay half-concealed under the dust ruffle. Succumbing to temptation, she reached for it, glad to feel its weight in her hand again. The blade threw lamplight in her eyes, dazzling.

So Morgana had made this. The hilt was very plain, just silver, but the sword as a whole was a spare, graceful work of art. She no longer felt any pain when she touched it, just a warmth that ran up her arm.

On impulse she got up and padded downstairs to the living-room bookcase, and searched until she found the title she was looking for. Tucking the book under her arm she went back to her bedroom.

The Legend of King Arthur. She opened it and began to read. Some time later she shut the book with a thoughtful expression.

So. According to legend, Arthur had been the son of King

Uther Pendragon of the Island of Britain, and Ygraine, who was originally another king's wife. There seemed to have been a lot of kings back then, all fighting each other. When Arthur was born, a red dragon appeared in the sky, and the rival kings vowed to kill the child who had been born under such a powerful portent. King Uther gave the child into the keeping of the wizard Merlin. Merlin himself had had a somewhat rocky beginning, it seemed, since when he was born it was rumored that he was not human but the son of a demon. But he had grown to be a wise and powerful wizard.

Arthur had been raised by a foster family in ignorance of his true identity. On the day Uther died a vast stone, four-square (whatever that meant), had appeared in a church-yard, and on that stone was an anvil, and in the anvil was a sword. Written on the blade in Latin was, "Whoso pulleth this sword out of this stone and wedge of steel is rightwise born King of all Britain."

Eleven kings, and plenty of other people, had had a go at the sword without luck. But when Arthur, a mere squire, put his hand on it, it came out easily. So everyone knew he was the rightful king, and that was that.

Alys tilted the blade on her knees to look at it again. No Latin, just the name. She felt at once disappointed and somehow relieved.

Gazing at the cover illustration of Merlin, a gray-bearded old man who looked wise and rather stern, Alys felt suddenly sleepy. She tucked the sword back under the dust ruffle and stretched out again, closing her eyes.

▾   ▾   ▾

Under a night sky thick with stars, far away from any city lights, Morgana Shee woke and automatically made a rapid check of the wards that protected her.

Yes, this place was still safe. If *she* entered, or even came near, Morgana would have warning. Feeling a faint tingling in her arm, she glanced at the heavy copper bracelet she wore, but the crystal was still whole, unshattered. So the children were safe as well. What, then, had caused her to wake? What caused this feeling of unease?

She could find no answer. Laying the Gold Staff close by she composed herself again for sleep. Memories, some pleasant, some not so pleasant, rose up to swim before her mind. Presently, she began to dream.

▼　▼　▼

Alys was dreaming, too. She knew she was dreaming, but she could not control what was happening. She could not even control herself. In fact, she was not herself, she was someone else, someone strange and familiar. . . .

Of course! How silly of her not to have realized. She was Morgana the sorceress, called by some Morgana of the Sidhe, wielder of a Gold Staff, and she was *absolutely furious*—

▼　▼　▼

Morgana strove to keep her voice calm as she addressed the young man before her. It never did any good to let Merlin know you were angry; he only enjoyed it.

"What you have done is evil," she said, wondering even as she said it if the term had any meaning for him. Like her, Merlin was half Quislai and half human. Such half-breeds were unusual; in fact, there were no records of any others.

It was not uncommon for a human to fall in love with one of the beautiful, unfathomable Faerie breed, but few children were ever born of such unions, and fewer still survived. Morgana's own life was a case in point. For many years— she would never know how many—she had lived at the side of her Quislai mother, wandering between the worlds and riding the Wild Hunt, scarcely aging, remaining eternally a child.

Then, as always happened sooner or later with the Quislai, her mother had misplaced her, or forgotten about her, and left her behind in a wilderness in the human world. A Quislai child, being immortal, would not have come to harm, but Morgana was not a full Quislai. She would have died if a human had not found her and taken her home and given her food and drink and a fire. And it was then, with her first taste of human food, that she had begun to age.

She had come to love her adoptive father. But she was always different. When a sorcerer of the Wildworld passed through her village he knew her heritage at once, and sent word to the Weerul Council. From that point on, the Council had taken charge of her, allowing her to study the Wild Arts as an apprentice. But even they were astonished—and not pleased—when the ragged halfling won a Gold Staff at the great contest. Worse still, she did not even need the Elixir of Days to extend her life, as the sorcerei did. Her Quislai blood kept her young, and though she was not immortal no one could tell how long she might live. Understandably, the sorcerei were wary of Morgana. She had no kin in the Wildworld, belonged to none of the great houses.

She was neither human nor Quislai, not entirely a sorceress. There was no place for her in their world.

So Morgana chose to live in the other one. She found humans to be generally unreliable, often dangerous, and sometimes cruel. The brevity of their lives made their passions hot and their perspective narrow. And yet among them she had a place. Even those that feared her, needed her; she filled a niche in their view of the world. At a time when many of the other Wildfolk were retreating uneasily from human civilization, she stayed and represented magic.

Merlin was in much the same position. Born to a human mother, he had been in less danger of being accidentally mislaid, but danger had come from another source. The midwife who tended his mother ran from the room shrieking that she had helped deliver a changeling. No human newborn was so eerily beautiful, no human child had hair the color of moonlight and silver eyes. The townspeople had come close to putting mother and child to death, and though he was allowed to live he grew up as one apart. Word of him reached the Weerul Council while he was still a boy and they had reluctantly consented to let him undergo apprenticeship as Morgana had. Their misgivings were well founded, for when the time came and another Gold Staff was offered in competition, the boy named Merlin claimed it.

And if Morgana had difficulty in fitting herself to Weerul society, Merlin was worse. He had incomparable talents—which he used at whim, for no fixed purpose, and certainly not on the Council's behalf. He laughed at custom and tradition. He did not even keep a house in the Wildworld, but instead went back to his native village. When he did visit Findahl it was mainly to wander through Chaotic Zones, areas of magic so wild and unpredictable they usually killed anyone but full Quislai. In fact, he behaved very much like a Quislai, except that he had power such as no Quislai had ever held. He had a Gold Staff.

And unfortunately, thought Morgana, looking at him now, he had the human ability to plan and to strategize, which no full Quislai ever had, either. He had ambition. She wondered what on earth was going on at this moment behind those beautiful, unfathomable silver eyes.

"It was wrong, Merlin," she said again quietly.

He put a hand over his heart and bowed. "I merely obeyed the orders of Uther, my master. These are times of war—"

"It was not war to clothe Uther in King Gorlois's likeness and send him to Ygraine so disguised! She thought it was her husband come back—and all the while her husband was lying dead on the field of battle."

"Slain by Uther's hand," agreed Merlin modestly. "I helped a bit—the mist cast round the field was mine—"

"Chaos take your mist," Morgana interrupted fiercely. "Merlin, listen to me for once. I tell you that you will not do such a thing again."

"There is no need." The young man smiled cheerfully and laced his fingers over his stomach. "Uther has conquered Cornwall already. Ygraine was his price, you see. He has been mad with love for her since he first beheld her six years ago. He was not eager to wage war until I swore to help him win her."

Morgana shut her eyes, feeling sick. She whispered, "How can you so misuse your powers?"

He repeated the bow. "I am reproved."

"You are irresponsible and mad," she said flatly. "But, mark me, you will do no further harm to Ygraine. She is a brave and gentle lady, and she and all her line are under my protection. Also . . . she is my friend."

Ygraine was one of the few truly noble people Morgana had ever met. She was valiant, honest, and generous to a fault. Moreover, she was one of the few humans who neither feared magic nor desired to turn it to her own ends, but wished merely to live in harmony with it. Morgana seldom interfered in human affairs—and especially not in politics or human conflict—but she was willing to break the custom of centuries now, to protect Ygraine.

"Very well," said Merlin equably. "I assure you, madam, I have never wished her harm."

Absurd as it was, he seemed perfectly sincere about that. Morgana shook her head at him wearily.

"Merlin, why?" she said. "Why do you do it? Why play at politics on this lonely island? If your mind turns that way you could have a leading voice on the Council. Here, you can only serve. And your master may be bold and ruthless, but he is a very *little* king."

Merlin's smile was far away. "I know. But his son will be a greater one."

"What do you mean? What son?"

"The child Ygraine carries now. The child of Ygraine and Uther. The blood of both runs in his veins and he will be a king such as this world has never known. He will rule all of Britain."

"All of *what?*"

"Britain. Not Albany or Cornwall or Logris, but an empire embracing all of them. All the kingdoms united. It does not exist yet, but it will. He will bring it together, and with my aid he will hold it. And it will be the greatest empire in this world one day, and his name will never be forgotten. You see, Morgana"—all at once the silver-eyed sorcerer suddenly looked very young and almost haunted—"I see things. Things that are not yet, but will be. I cannot help it. And I have seen this."

Morgana said dryly, "He will have to be an extraordinary man, indeed."

"He will. But he must be prepared for the task. And that is why," he added, almost offhandedly, "he is to be given into my keeping. Uther has already agreed."

"Are you mad? What has Uther to do with it? The child—if there is a child, which I doubt—is Ygraine's. You could not take it from her. Should you even try I would call in the Council."

"You?"

"Yes, I! They would interfere for that, they would not allow it. *I* would not allow it."

The silver eyes, so vulnerable a moment ago, flamed with passion. "I must have the child! I must! He cannot be trained like an ordinary king. He needs to learn things only I can teach him—no, not sorcery, but how to see the world through different eyes. He must be innocent of the petty quarrels of his fathers. He must be *mine.*"

Morgana said coldly, "You will not have him."

For a moment or so Merlin looked wild. Then a change seemed to come over him; he paused, as if listening to distant music, and then he calmed himself. At last he smiled his brief, flashing smile.

"Very well," he said to Morgana. "I make you this bargain. You do not wish me to take the child against Ygraine's desire. And I tell you, that if when I come to take him, Ygraine says even one word in protest, I will not."

Morgana looked at him with mistrust. "I will send to the Council for a Feathered Serpent to be present at the birth. You will be held to your word."

Merlin said simply, "I agree."

▾   ▾   ▾

The Council did indeed send a Feathered Serpent, an arbiter of justice, to assure that no treachery was done. But Merlin was able to keep his word. Ygraine died in childbirth and was able to speak no word of protest when he came to claim her son.

Morgana herself stood by, cold with grief and anger but helpless, as the gray-cloaked figure appeared and took the child from the queen's lifeless arms. For a moment Merlin cradled him, then he touched the very top of the tiny head with his lips.

The sorceress felt some of her fury ebb away, to be replaced by bewilderment. Her voice shook a little when she spoke.

"He is still of Ygraine's line, and under my protection. Be

sure you do him no hurt, Merlin. Be very sure."

The young man raised his silver eyes, startled, as if he had forgotten she was still in the room. His surprise and affront seemed genuine.

"Hurt him? This is Arthur of Britain," he said, as if that were answer enough. Then he cast his gray cloak around himself and the baby and was gone.

The legends about Arthur began that night. Rumor spread that Ygraine had given birth to an heir in the lonely tower at Tintagel where she had cloistered herself since the death of her husband, Gorlois, and at midnight a great dragon, red and black in the moonlight, was seen to spread its wings and burst from the battlements. The Feathered Serpent was returning to the Council. But the simple folk in the town below took it as a sign and were filled with wonder and fear. A very great king—son of the dragon— must have been born.

The Council was satisfied that no treachery had been done, but Morgana was not. At that time she lived on an island in the enclosed Sea of Cornwall, near the Forest of Darnantes. The inhabitants of the region knew of her presence on the "lake" and wove legends around it, but seldom had any dealings with her. Every so often some of them would venture out in a small boat with gifts or a plea for help, where they would row in confusion and befuddlement until she took pity on them and guided them through the mists. If there was sickness or drought in the village she sometimes lent aid, and if her peace was disturbed for no reason she could be swift in anger, but otherwise she and the villagers did not disturb one another. But in these troubled days she made it a point to hire messengers and keep herself abreast of all Merlin's doings.

What she found left her puzzled and pleased. Merlin seemed at last to have forsaken his wild ways and to have found a purpose. He had given the baby to a very decent country family to raise and from all reports the child was growing strong and healthy, learning hunting lore and swordsmanship, but no statecraft. And of course, thought Morgana, learning whatever lessons Merlin deemed it necessary to teach him. In any case, the boy had come to no ill, and while his father continued to wage war and bicker over borders with his neighbors, Arthur reached young manhood in happy ignorance of his own lineage.

He was sixteen years of age when Uther died. Rival kings and warlords at once began to quarrel with one another over the late king's lands, and civil war seemed certain. Morgana, who had relaxed her vigilance in watching Merlin some time ago, now wondered with dry humor how the young sorcerer intended to convince anyone that Arthur was even the rightful king of Logris, much less of this mythical empire he spoke of. She could see no way for Arthur to claim his throne without bloodshed.

The answer came quickly, and already wrapped in the glamour of legend. A great rock had appeared in a square in London, and on the rock was an anvil of steel, and imbedded in the anvil was the point of a sword. The words on the blade could be read clearly and proclaimed that whoever should draw the sword from the anvil was rightwise born king of Britain. So far, many had tried to draw the sword out, but none could do so.

It was a very neat trick, and Morgana admired it. Merlin always had had a flair for dramatics. An air of expectancy fell over the kingdom as all waited for the true heir to be revealed. When at last Arthur was brought to London by his foster family and induced to try his hand, he succeeded in full view of the assembled populace. It was beautifully staged and perfectly executed, and Arthur's claim was established beyond dispute. The rival nobles withdrew.

Morgana heard this and was relieved. So far Merlin had kept his word to the letter, and had behaved not only sensibly, but even honorably. She began to feel that perhaps she had misjudged him.

But that, of course, was before she saw the sword with her own eyes, and understood what he had done. . . .

▼ ▼ ▼

In a human forest far away in time as well as space from the island near Darnantes, Morgana Shee came awake with a start and jumped up. The vivid dream, which had been like a walk in memory, disappeared from her mind. This was no time for dreaming. *She* was near, the wards were thrumming with suppressed energy. She had not found Morgana yet, nor indeed the other thing she sought, but she was close enough to be a threat.

A faint smile touched the lips of the little sorceress standing in the moonlight. Now, what shall we have for a distraction, she thought: fire or flood or wild beasts? Not an earthquake, that would do more damage than it was worth.

She laid light fingers on the Gold Staff and above her lightning flashed and crackled in the sky.

▼ ▼ ▼

Alys woke and started, too, flinging off her covers. Her mind was full of strange things, which dissolved even as she tried to grasp them. Her right arm was one solid blaze of pain, as if she had been wrestling all night with some great enemy.

She stumbled to the window and pulled the drapes open, looking out. For an instant, on the moonlit lawn below, she caught a glimpse of something dark and shining and thought she heard a loud, wet smack. But then it was gone and she wondered if it had ever really been there.

Wincing and rubbing her arm, she fell back on the bed. On the floor the sword caught a stray glint of moonlight, which quickly dimmed as the sky outside darkened with clouds. Alys pulled up the covers and went back to sleep almost at once, this time without dreaming at all.

The Dark Thing

The next morning the skies over Villa Park were thick with clouds that seemingly couldn't make up their minds whether or not to rain, but instead grudgingly released a continuous hazy drizzle which depressed everyone who saw it. Alys woke with a stiff neck and a headache, and wished she could just stay in bed.

Cold water on her face and cold orange juice in a glass revived her a little, but in the back of her mind lurked images which would not quite come to the surface, images which disturbed her. She could not tell if they were memories or dreams or memories of dreams, but they haunted her.

Her arm cramped when she moved it. Feeling dull and heavy, she helped the others make breakfast and get off to school. Her own performance in class that day was of the least inspired kind.

After school they all met at Morgana's where Alys began reading to Charles and Janie from her book about King Arthur. She had carried it around with her all day and felt somehow compelled to keep returning to it. It seemed to hold secrets.

In the kitchen Claudia was reading, as well, to the vixen. This usually worked out all right because though Claudia was a poor reader, the vixen was worse. Claudia told most of the story from the pictures, anyway, the way she had in kindergarten.

But today the vixen wasn't listening. She was pacing back and forth along the counter under the kitchen window, the gold of her collar gleaming dully against her red fur. She went very quickly, almost running, to the end of the counter, then swung without slowing to go the other way. It disturbed Claudia. It reminded her for some reason of the mongoose she had seen at the Los Angeles Zoo, which had paced endlessly from one end of its cage to the other, never slackening speed to glance at the people who were looking curiously in at it.

Claudia closed the book. The vixen did not seem to notice.

"Maybe . . . maybe I should read this another time. Maybe tomorrow. We could do something else. . . ."

The vixen stopped, but she was not looking at Claudia. She was staring out the window, at a sky billowing with clouds so dark they were almost blue. Droplets of moisture had collected on the glass.

Claudia hugged the book to her, feeling strangely uneasy. She had never seen the vixen act this way before.

"Is something wrong?" she asked hesitantly. "If something's wrong I could go get Alys . . ."

The vixen made no reply.

"I guess I should go, then," said Claudia humbly. "I guess you want to be alone."

After another minute of silence, she rose to leave.

"Too many years!"

The vixen's voice was strange and hoarse. Claudia froze

where she was, and the vixen turned. She went on speaking in that rough, new voice.

"Too many years, too many centuries! Living with humans, surrounded by humans. Eating their dead food. Sleeping inside walls!"

Claudia stroked the corner of the book with her fingers, her mouth dry.

"And surrounded by *things!* Square things, flat things, rectangular things. Everything with a *shape.* All smooth and hard, with cold unliving smells. All *made.* "

The vixen began to pace again.

"This was good land once. Wooded. You could run for hours, days without hearing the sound of a human voice. How long has it been since I have been out of the range of a human voice? Now I hunt in vacant lots. In peoples' very backyards, for the scavengers that live on their garbage!"

Claudia whispered, "I'm sorry," but the vixen went on, unheeding.

"Many animals do that. But where is *my* den scratched out in the soft earth? Where are my cubs? Where is the mate to stand beside me and share my triumph when the rabbit's spine snaps and the rich blood flows?" The vixen's sides were heaving like a bellows, her ears back. "Nowhere! I have no den, no mate, no cubs. Because I have been *civilized.* I have been tamed. I am a pet fox."

"I'm sorry," said Claudia again, numbly. It was all she could think of to say. She wanted to leave. She didn't want to hear any more.

"Claudia!"

Claudia kept walking.

"Human child!"

Claudia stopped, drawing her head down between her shoulders, and turned.

"Come here," said the vixen. She was standing on the counter, tail low and straight, her eyes like golden orbs, her ribs still heaving. Claudia slowly, against her will, took a step.

"Come here," said the vixen, "and take this damned thing off my neck."

▾   ▾   ▾

Presently, Alys missed her youngest sister.

"She's with the vixen in the kitchen. You know, Alys," Charles added with a grimace, "if you ask me, the vixen is getting kind of weird. When I got here this afternoon she was just running out of the henhouse—and I don't think she was in there counting eggs. When she saw me she turned and ran the other way."

"But just yesterday she was furious because Talisman—" Alys broke off. "I suppose it *was* Talisman?" There was a silence. Alys rubbed her forehead. "Huh. All right, I'll talk to her."

The kitchen door was closed, which was unusual. Alys opened it and stopped dead.

Claudia was standing by the open window, her cheeks wet. On the counter, unclasped, was the vixen's golden collar.

"She's gone, Alys," said Claudia, raising a tear-stained face. "She's gone away with Talisman."

"Oh, Claudia!"

"Oh, great," said Charles from behind.

Alys took Claudia in her arms, looking over her sister's

brown head at the open window. A fine mist of rain was blowing in.

"She—she said she was tired of being *civilized.* . . ."

"She'll come back," said Alys, closing the window, and knowing as she said it that she was not at all sure the vixen would.

Claudia cried silently, burying her face in Alys's shoulder, and Alys knew she knew, too.

She let her cry a little, then said:

"Come on. I'll make you some cocoa."

Claudia sat up, still sniffling.

"No. I just want to—to be by myself for a little."

"All right. But stay here. Don't go home without us." Alys had decided that from now on none of the four of them should go anywhere alone, but she didn't want to frighten Claudia by saying that.

Claudia nodded mechanically, her head bowed. Alys shut the door on her.

▾ ▾ ▾

Claudia sat for some minutes, then got up and opened the window again. Alys, she knew, was grieved and angry at the vixen's departure. But with Claudia it went deeper than grief or anger. She simply could not accept it. She wanted to rewind the whole afternoon and erase it, then start again. Her vision blurred as tears welled up in her eyes.

Maybe—maybe the vixen had not gone to Talisman yet. Maybe she was just outside somewhere, and if Claudia could find her she could make her listen.

Alys wouldn't let her go out in the rain. So she didn't tell

Alys. She boosted herself through the open window and let herself down onto the wet grass.

Outside the drizzle was turning into a shower. Far away there was a rumble of thunder, as if the sky were in sympathy with Claudia's feelings. The ground smelled of rich damp earth and molding leaves.

Shielding her eyes with her hand, she began walking, away from the wooded grounds of the estate that were usually the vixen's territory, toward Irvine Park. There was no movement on Center Street. The rain had driven all humans inside and all animals under shelter. A great silence surrounded her as she turned down Churchill Lane.

Thunder grumbled again and rain pattered into her face. Her clothes were wet. Claudia lowered her hand and stood unprotected, not caring.

A whisper of sound on the other side of a fence made her look up. Something dark was moving along the fencetop underneath a big overhanging tree in the corner. The rain and the drooping branches screened the animal. Claudia made a hopeful greeting sound and held out her arms.

The thing came closer, hesitantly, it seemed. Claudia reached her arms up higher, narrowing her eyes against the rain. If it was a cat, it was a very big one. In fact—much too big—but a dog wouldn't walk the top of a fence—or move with such rippling grace—

Claudia stood frozen as the creature edged out of the shadowing branches of the tree, putting one foot in front of another deliberately—except that it didn't have feet—it had *hands*—

A thin shriek broke from Claudia's lips. She turned and fled blindly down Churchill Lane. She reached the cul-de-sac at the end and turned, panting, to look behind her.

Through sheets of rain she saw something dark and sinuous drop down onto the street.

Claudia whirled and looked at the house before her in panic. She knew what to do if someone was chasing her; she had been taught in school. Without hesitation she ran up the porch steps and pounded on the door with both fists.

There was no answer. She kept pounding and rang the doorbell, looking with wild eyes over her shoulder. She didn't know what the thing was, but it was *bad*. Every instinct told her she was in danger. At last, in desperation, she tried the knob—it would not turn.

She splashed back down the steps, cutting across the front garden and floundering in the mud where marigolds and dahlias had just been planted. One look at the next house and she pulled up short. There was something on the porch, crouched and waiting.

Claudia backed up stiffly. The dark shape rose on its legs and took one slow step toward her. Her next step back brought her up against wooden boards that gave slightly. Without taking her eyes off the thing she reached back. Her fingers encountered the wet, fibrous roughness of twine.

The dark shape took another slow step, and stopped. She was still well out of range of any normal predator. But Claudia knew animals, knew the tiny signs by which they betrayed themselves. She knew the dilation of pupils that meant a cat was about to strike, and she knew by the way this creature gathered itself that it was going to spring. She gave the cord a yank and twisted inside, slamming the gate shut in the same motion. She heard a soggy thud as the creature landed where she had been standing a moment ago.

She backed away from the gate, hands pressed over her mouth. She couldn't run anymore. At the top of the fence appeared two soft, wrinkled black hands. They gripped to bear weight, and Claudia found she could run after all.

She stumbled against an outdoor barbecue, recoiled, and tripped over a piece of rawhide twisted into a bone. Recovering, she made for the far end of the fence, with no clear goal except to put as much distance between herself and the thing as possible. There was a noise behind her. Her head snapped around, her foot missed a step on the patio. She fell heavily, landing on knees and palms. A shape surged up beside her and she screamed, gazing at it in wide-eyed terror.

Then the lolling tongue, white teeth, and chocolate-drop eyes came into focus. It was a dog, her dog, the dog she'd used to send a message to Janie. Her letter dog.

To Claudia's enormous credit, her first impulse was to warn it away. She waved scraped hands and made a gobbling sound, incomprehensible in any language, human or canine, with this intent. The dog, which had been expressing its joy and surprise at finding her, and proclaiming its willingness to undertake another mission, preferably a dangerous one, became suddenly alert. Ears went up, tail and body froze, eyes locked on a dark shape across the yard. The hair on its back rose stiffly, lips drew away from teeth, and a low, throbbing growl began somewhere inside its chest. The growl rose in pitch and volume and suddenly exploded in a volley of harsh barking.

Claudia found herself sitting, arms flung around the setter's chest, feeling the barking as well as hearing it. The dark shape by the fence seemed to hesitate, then a hand stretched out as it took a step nearer. The barking subsided into growls again as Claudia, clutching desperately, jabbered an explanation. One concept, and one alone, seemed to get through to the setter. This was an intruder, a trespasser of the worst kind, who was violating not only the setter's territory but the setter's world. It was anathema, it was worse than cats-rats-and-postmen. It was to be gotten rid of. The setter threw back his head and sounded the alarm.

Claudia started back at the sound. This was not barking, it was a cry which showed how close dogs really are under the skin to their cousins the wolves. It was a howl. The setter was calling in the pack.

The sound carried superbly, even in the mist-deadened air. For blocks around, in many tones, rose the answer.

On Jocotol Avenue a sleek square Labrador retriever vaulted out into the rain while his astonished owner stared after him over two dripping bags of groceries. Two doors away a pair of miniature poodles began to dig frantically at the window screen, yapping shrilly. A bulldog from Smokewood Drive calmly pushed his gate a certain way and trotted purposefully off. A collie thrust first her nose, then her head, and, with a final lunge, her entire body through a loose board in her fence.

The clamor increased as the cry was passed from house to house. At Amate Circle a Kerry blue terrier took a running leap and cleared a five-foot fence almost without touching it. Sharon Lane contributed two beagles and a sheepdog mix. On Lemon Street a Great Dane, baying wildly, hurled himself once too often against a sliding glass door, which finally exploded outward in a satisfying burst of glass shards.

From near and far they came. Claudia, with one hand buried in the setter's rusty fur, watched and listened in amazement. Dogs were vaulting over the fence, scrabbling at the gate, barking and howling from the street. Every so often the head of a tiny but determined schnauzer would appear above the fence from the yard next door, give a fierce yap, and then disappear as it fell again. The bulldog and the Kerry blue had begun to circle the dark shape, which had pulled back but did not look beaten yet. One of the beagles darted in low and jumped back with a mouthful of fur.

"Oh, be careful," said Claudia, but just then there was a heavy thump and the gate crashed in entirely. On top of it was an enormous Great Dane shaking its head and wearing a foolish expression. It saw the dark thing and forgot about being embarrassed. It leaped. All the other dogs took this as a signal, and sprang almost in unison, piling on.

The dark thing extricated itself from the canine pileup and gained the top of the fence in a bound, where the schnauzer, astonished by its good fortune, got in one swift nip before gravity took over. Extending spiderlike legs, the dark shape scuttled away.

In the yard the setter tilted his nose to the sky and howled triumph. Some of the other dogs, notably the Lab and the Dane, began to roll in the mud to work off their exuberance. In a spirit of pure camaraderie they began to roll on Claudia, too.

▾   ▾   ▾

"Did you hear something?" Janie raised her head as Alys paused between pages.

"Only thunder. Why?"

"I don't know. I thought I heard a dog barking. This house is so isolated and the walls are so thick you usually can't hear anything from outside."

Alys shut the book, feeling uneasy. "I think I'd better get Claudia. I don't like her being alone in there so long."

There was a period of great confusion following the opening of the kitchen door. It ended with Alys, Charles, and Janie running down the driveway just as Claudia, the setter, and their muddy entourage came marching up it.

"I ought to smack you," said Alys, when Claudia had gulped out the whole story. She hugged her instead. The only clean places on Claudia's face were the tear trails on her cheeks and she looked stunned and shaken. "Okay, everybody, that's it. We're going home, and we stay inside the wards all night tonight. Nobody leaves."

The dogs dispersed as the children walked their bikes back. When they reached their own porch only the setter was left; it waited until Claudia was safely indoors to trot off. As it rounded the corner it met the two miniature poodles, which had finally torn a hole in the screen and gotten out. It gave them a patronizing glance and went on by without stopping. Typical, the sway of its tail seemed to say. Always late.

Alys, watching from the doorway, smiled in spite of herself. As she turned to go inside she saw the sky.

"Look, oh look! Oh, Janie, come quick and see!"

It had appeared from nowhere, a great arch of light against the midnight blue clouds. The colors were so vibrant that the whole thing almost looked solid, except near the ground where she could see red- and green-tinted hills through the base. It reached halfway up the sky, squarely spanning Villa Park.

Janie glanced at it mechanically, and did a double take.

"What's wrong?" Alys felt almost cross as she said it. Trust Janie to spoil a vision of beauty.

"It's upside down."

"How can you say that? It's perfect."

Janie smiled, looking patient and grim. "Alys, do you know how rainbows are formed? Droplets of water in the air break white light up into the spectrum of colors. And each color of light has a certain wavelength, which determines where it appears in the rainbow. Red light gets bent the least, so it appears on top. The other colors appear in this order: orange, yellow, green, blue, and violet. It's a law of nature, a matter of physics. Now do you want to look at that rainbow and tell me the order of the colors?"

"Violet . . ." Alys's voice trailed off and she had to clear her throat and start again. "Violet, blue, green, yellow, orange, and red. Oh."

They stood silently. The wind changed direction and they both felt the chill of fine rain.

"But, Janie, that wouldn't be caused by things getting through the Passage, would it?" Janie shook her head. "Then what do you think it is?"

"I think if it's a joke somebody has an odd sense of humor. And they've gone to a lot of trouble, and . . . they have power to spare. Other than that, I honestly don't know. But I'm scared."

▾   ▾   ▾

The Second Dream

"Finish telling us about King Arthur," said Charles after dinner.

"Isn't there anything on television?"

Charles missed the sarcasm entirely. "The TV's on the fritz again. Nothing but static."

Janie and Alys looked at one another. Claudia was drinking a glass of milk at the table, looking pale and sad but otherwise unharmed. Janie shook her head slightly and shrugged.

"Wards are up and safe," she murmured.

Alys nodded. "All right," she said to Charles. "We might as well have hot cocoa if we're going to have stories. And it's your turn to make it. And not the instant kind."

They sat around the fireplace, cupping steaming mugs. Alys told them what she had read while Claudia looked at the pictures.

"So, Arthur was the crowned king, and he was the best king anybody had ever known even though he was so young. He gathered together all the best knights, the strongest and bravest, and they all sat as equals at the Round Table. Everybody thought that he was crazy at first, and that the knights would only fight each other, but they didn't. They went out and righted wrongs and slew evil monsters and things.

"And all this time Arthur was guided by Merlin the enchanter, who was the wisest and the most farsighted . . ." Alys trailed off, not even aware that she had stopped speaking. There was something strange tugging at her memory.

"Yes? Go on," said Charles.

"Uh . . . the wisest wizard in the land, he was," said Alys, hearing a notable lack of conviction in her own voice. "And, uh, one day he took Arthur out riding and they came to a lake, and they saw a hand holding a sword sticking out of the lake. Arthur asked who the sword belonged to and Merlin said, the Lady of the Lake. Then a beautiful woman appeared and gave the sword to Arthur, and it was a magic sword, and he always used it after that. Because his other one, the one he'd pulled out of the stone, had gotten broken or something. And this new sword was called Excalibur. . . ."

Once again Alys's voice trailed off. Then she looked at Janie, eyes widening. "Excalibur . . . *Excalibur* . . ."

"Or Caliborn. Depending on your source. Yes."

"You mean I've got *Excalibur* upstairs under my bed?"

"It's a funny place to put it, but you've got it, all right. Now you see why I wasn't sure about—"

"But, listen," interrupted Alys. "If Morgana made that sword, then Morgana must have been the Lady of the Lake. But I thought she was Morgan LeFay, and she fought against the Knights of the Round Table."

"Don't believe everything you hear," said Janie severely. "And I've told you, Morgana has had lots of names. Some legends don't tell the whole story."

"What legends don't tell what whole story?" Charles complained. "I haven't heard any of this."

Alys spoke slowly. "According to tradition, Morgan LeFay was a powerful, evil enchantress. She plotted against Arthur's knights, and bewitched them every chance she could. She and Merlin were sworn enemies. But—do you mean, Janie, that Morgana didn't really plot against Arthur and Merlin? Or—"

"I'm saying that maybe she had her reasons. I would have thought," Janie added, looking at her oddly, "that *you* would know more about it than I do."

"What on earth do you mean by that?" said Alys, but some part of her knew exactly what Janie meant. She *did* know, if only she could remember—

The sudden jerk of the ground took her by surprise. For an instant she thought it was something going on inside *her*, a wave of dizziness, but she quickly realized the truth.

"Get under the doorways, quick!"

The whole house was shaking. They crouched under the frames of the doorways, Alys with Claudia and Charles with Janie, and watched each other with frightened eyes.

"Look at the chandelier," said Charles. It was swinging back and forth, crystal pendants tinkling musically. The sliding doors to the closet rattled. Ornaments fell off shelves, and suddenly, with a crash, so did a row of books. Claudia shrieked, and Janie leaned her head on her knees, looking ill.

And then it was over. Alys made them sit in the doorways a few minutes to make sure. When they got up their legs were so rubbery it felt as if the room were still moving.

"Guess it was an aftershock," mumbled Janie.

"And now maybe *more* things have come through the Passage?" demanded Alys. Janie spread her hands helplessly; she didn't know.

"Look," said Alys, "do you really think all these creatures are just things that came through the Passage? The shape on the roof, and the bobcat, and the thing that chased Claudia?"

"I never said *any* of those things came through the Passage. I just said *something* did."

"Well, I don't think it was any of these." She hadn't realized this until she said it.

"Where did they come from, then?" demanded Charles. "And what are they doing? Why are they bothering us?"

There was a silence. Alys was thinking about the rainbow.

"I don't know," she said at last. "But, Janie, I want you to check the wards again. I feel as if something were about to happen."

The wards were up and untouched. Still, Alys couldn't shake off her feeling of apprehension as she went to bed. She took the sword out and held it a long time before placing it on the nightstand. At last she fell asleep.

And immediately began to dream.

▾   ▾   ▾

When Morgana went to Arthur's chief palace at Caerleon to look at him with her own eyes she did so inconspicuously, taking only a small retinue. She had had many servants over the years, for her lifetime spanned many human generations. She would take on an attendant young and raw, full of little quirks that annoyed her, and almost before she knew

89

it would wake to find a retainer well loved and trusted, but growing old. It saddened her.

Her only constant companion was the vixen. One day when she was still an apprentice she had gone to the woods to gather herbs and found a tiny fox cub which had been savaged by some animal. Morgana's heart had gone out to the little creature, and she brought it home to heal by sorcery. By the time it was well it followed her everywhere. The Council had been shocked when she used her portion of the Elixir of Days—which could not, by law, be denied to her once she won her staff—to grant her familiar long life, but Morgana had never regretted it.

Now, traveling to Caerleon, she took only the vixen and two maidservants. One was named Viviane, a slender girl with a steady gaze and hair like copper. She had a gift for sorcery, and Morgana encouraged it, for although it was difficult for a human to win a staff, it was not impossible.

They watched Arthur from concealment and Morgana was pleased with what she saw. He was a tall and handsome youth, with a strong easy step and an air of energy and authority. The gold threads in his tunic were no brighter than his hair, and his eyes were as blue as the gems in the hilt of his sword.

But, looking at those gems, Morgana's eyes fell on one, a blue stone the size of a walnut, and a cold wind seemed to go through her. Where it had come from, she could not imagine, but no sorceress could mistake it. It was one of the Forgotten Gems, one of the stones of great power whose fate was lost in the mists of antiquity. Great power—and great peril. Its name was Mirror of Heaven, but there was nothing heavenly about its influence. A fury came over her, and she cast a portal straight into Merlin's tower room in the castle to demand an explanation.

Merlin smiled at her. "I don't remember where I got it," he said. "I found it lying about somewhere."

If Elwyn had said this, Morgana would have believed it. But not Merlin.

"What do you mean by giving such a thing to a human?" she said. "Have you lost your wits entirely? Or are you merely trying to destroy him?"

Merlin raised an insulted eyebrow. "It will not destroy him but protect him. He will be almost invulnerable—"

"To weapons of steel, perhaps. But what wild magic is inside that stone, to prey upon his mind? Merlin"—she leaned forward—"the Council itself could not contain the power of those Gems. They were made right before the Time of Chaos, and some say all that happened after was their doing. Or have you forgotten your history as well?"

Merlin simply smiled maddeningly. "Ah, the old tales. What a pity so few of them are true. For what it's worth, you have my leave to try to take the sword from Arthur. I don't think he'll give it to you, though. It was a gift from me."

Merlin actually brought Arthur to the Forest of Darnantes himself. Morgana watched them riding toward her, laughing and talking, the sun shining on the silver hair of the one and the gold of the other. They looked for all the world like two carefree young knights on holiday.

Leaving Merlin on the shore, she took Arthur across the lake into her house. There, with both hands, she held out an object wrapped in dark green silk.

He unwrapped it and drew in his breath quickly. She could see the wonder in his eyes when he raised them to her.

"It is the most beautiful sword I have ever seen," he said simply, sitting and laying it across his knees.

"It is yours," said Morgana. "I made it for you. But I ask one thing in return, that you give me the other."

Arthur grasped the hilt of the sword at his belt and Morgana had to control herself from wincing at the sight of his hand on the Gem. "Well?" she said.

Arthur's honest blue eyes—Ygraine's eyes—met hers regretfully. "I cannot," he said.

"Merlin has told you, I believe, why I want it."

"He has said that you fear it will work a great bane upon me, and upon those I love best. But, lady, this sword was given me by Merlin himself, and it is the sword of my kingship. He does not believe it will bring me any harm. But, regardless, I will take the adventure ordained me. I must not turn back from peril."

Morgana stared at him. Two things were clear to her even without the extra rapport the sword engendered between them: that Arthur was of a simplicity and purity of heart such as she had never encountered, and that he loved Merlin very much. Perhaps he believed he could conquer the evil in the stone as he meant, with absolute sincerity, to conquer all the evil in the world.

She bowed her head. "Your majesty," she said, and

stopped, and started again. "Arthur," she said, "there are some things quite beyond your powers."

"Yes, I know," he said steadily. "But if no one ever tries to strive against them no one will ever succeed. We must simply do our best, you know. And hope."

Morgana dropped her eyes. "Promise me one thing, at least, for the sake of the love I bore your mother. If you will not give up the sword, at least forbear to use it. You have another, now."

"And a fairer," he said, courteously. "I will do what you ask. I will lay the old one aside and give out that it is broken, and I will use your sword all my days. May I be shown worthy of it!" He kissed her hand and left.

Morgana watched him go and whispered, "Oh, Merlin, what have you done? And what are you yet to do?"

She feared very much that Arthur, with his innocence and inexperience, would come to disaster among the knights and rival warriors at his court. But the opposite was true: the young king somehow brought out the best in people, and soon champions from kingdoms far and near were coming to Caerleon to lay their weapons at his feet. Still, she was afraid. Arthur's knights seemed to take his philosophy to heart: refuse no adventure and suffer no injustice to endure, but *they* were not Arthur. They were ordinary men, with passions and jealousies of their own. They could be dangerous.

Meanwhile Merlin continued to amuse himself. Although he must have been at least partly responsible for Arthur's ideas, and although he continued to advise and support

Arthur in his efforts to unite the kingdoms of Britain, the presence of the Gem seemed to wake the Quislai in him, and there were times when he just couldn't resist a joke. It was he who sent two knights to slay a dread perilous monster in Morgana's lake, an adventure which ended with the death of her selkie, a gentle and domesticated pet like a seal. Morgana herself preferred not to kill unless it was unavoidable, so she confined herself to a spell which sent the knights running off into the forest, convinced they were wild boars. Still, this started a feud with the knights' relatives, and when that was settled, new warriors kept coming. Furious, she called Merlin to her.

"What have you told them of me, that they come here looking for battle?"

Merlin displayed round-eyed innocence. "Why, nothing—except that you are an enchantress. Which is only true. And perhaps one or two other things which I can't recall at the moment."

"And these one or two other things—were *they* true?"

Merlin thought hard. "I am not sure. *Do* you lure men to dance with you on the water and then drag them beneath the waves? And have you the bodies of twelve good knights hung upside down in your dungeon?"

Morgana repressed the impulse to shake him, and also, paradoxically, to laugh. He was completely irresponsible and quite beyond her understanding. But she had had enough experience in dealing with her half sister Elwyn, who shared these exact qualities, to know that reproaches would do no good.

"It must stop," she said flatly, laying a hand on her staff.

"Do you understand me, Merlin? It must stop at once."

She had, as a matter of fact, no real way of compelling him. His staff was as powerful as her own, and if she had experience to draw on, he could lay hands on a Gem with powers untold. But he agreed, and even seemed genuinely repentant.

As far as she could tell, he kept his word, but it made little difference in the end. Her reputation was already established, and many knights came to the lake girded for battle and went back to add to the tales of her beauty and wickedness. She tried to hurt them as little as possible.

Years passed. She saw Merlin's prophecies about Arthur come true. The kingdoms were united; Arthur became High King. He married Guinevere, a shy little princess from Wales. Warriors continued to flock to him. Morgana sent one of her own household, a bold and gallant young man named Lancelot whom she had fostered since his mother died, and he became Arthur's strong right hand.

The real trouble started then. Merlin had always been jealous of anyone who shared Arthur's affections, and it was difficult for him to accept that the boy who had depended on him could care for others as well. As time went on the young sorcerer seemed to find it harder to resist his darker impulses. The Gem, perhaps. One thing she knew he had done was start rumors that Lancelot du Lac and Queen Guinevere had betrayed the king. Arthur believed neither the rumors nor the reports that Merlin was behind them. He would hear no evil of the people he loved.

Morgana did not know what other harm the Gem was doing. Because of its influence or no, feuds and factions developed between the knights. Perhaps it simply was not possible to have so many powerful and independent lords under one roof without fomenting trouble. Still, somehow or other, by his very presence, Arthur held them all together.

Morgana, sensing his love and concern through the sword, wondered how long it could last.

Down in the Dark

Alys woke all at once and sat up in bed, overcome by a feeling of foreboding. At first the feeling was vague, and then it narrowed into a focus. Something had wakened her. She held herself quite still for several minutes, listening, then threw off the covers and got up. Her hand reached for the sword automatically; she didn't even have to glance down as she picked it up.

Half the lights in the house were still on downstairs, but this did nothing to make her feel more safe. Darkness hung in corners and pooled behind furniture. She made the circuit of quiet room after quiet room, her uneasiness growing with every step.

As she approached the dining room she faltered and pulled up short. The many lights in the room turned the sliding glass doors into half-mirrors which reflected the oak table and the chandelier, making it hard to see outside. But there *was* something outside, something moving, coming right up to the glass and then away again. Alys stared at it, her brow creasing, her eyes narrowing. She felt her hands slowly lower the sword.

It was Janie outside, wearing a white nightgown which fluttered around her bare ankles. She moved quickly and lightly up to the sliding glass doors, almost but not quite touching them as she cupped her hands around her face to peer in. Then she danced away again. She reminded Alys of some great, pale moth going blindly from window to window.

But Janie never wore nightgowns, she wore pajamas. And the face framed between those slender hands was blank, expressionless. Alys felt ice up and down her backbone. She took a step back.

The next instant she almost screamed aloud as something grabbed her from behind. She struggled and managed to get the sword up before she saw a tumble of black hair and wide purple eyes; then she froze in shock.

"Shhh!" Janie waited until Alys had taken a deep breath and nodded, indicating that the temptation to yell was over, before removing her hand from Alys's mouth. It really was Janie. She was wearing neither a nightgown nor pajamas, but rumpled jeans and a pullover. There was a red crease on one cheek—from falling asleep on a book, Alys guessed.

Slowly, as if compelled, Alys turned to look outside again. It was still there, bumbling against the glass.

"What in the name of heaven is it?"

"I don't know." Janie was looking, too, leaning over Alys's arm. She spoke in a whisper. "Offhand, three things come to mind: phantasm, elemental, or boojum."

"Boojum?"

Janie grimaced. "My word. It's a kind of sprite you can make by sorcery, by conjuring from an element. But I can't tell what that thing is, not without a closer look."

"Is it trying to get through the wards?"

Janie shook her head, looking disturbed. "The strange

thing is, the wards haven't given any warning at all. And I would have known if they had, I've been awake most of the night." She added, "Couldn't sleep. Busy reading."

But Alys, touched, knew the truth. Her sister, who looked at the moment like nothing so much as an undernourished elf in wrinkled denim, had been standing guard for all of them.

"Next time you tell me and we'll take turns," she said. She added, "What do you suggest we do now?"

Janie bit her lips, then her gaze dropped considerably to the sword. "We really should try and trap it, see what it's made of," she said, seeming reluctant. "Oh, I don't like doing this without Morgana."

"We don't seem to have much choice."

"No. All right, listen to me. We have to be careful; I don't know what that thing can do. And I need my rowan stick."

They conferred together in whispers. Then Alys crept around behind the dining table and stationed herself on one side of the sliding glass doors, while Janie crouched on the other. The beautiful, pale, blind thing continued to flutter up against the glass. Alys's eyes met Janie's; she saw her sister's lips move soundlessly and just as soundlessly counted with her: one, two, three, *now*. On the last count Janie brought the rowan wand down with a crack, breaking the wards, and Alys simultaneously jumped out, flipping up the lock on the door and pulling it open almost in one motion. The white-nightgowned thing tumbled inside and Janie threw the door closed again, restoring the wards as Alys dove in a tackle.

The nightgown was cool against her cheek as she locked

her arms about the Janie-thing's waist, and she could smell the freshness of night air in the folds of cotton. The intruder yielded and fell to the floor and she fell on top of it, momentarily concerned because it seemed so fragile. And then somehow everything went wrong. She found herself staring into blank, lovely violet eyes as the thing twisted with impossible agility and speed and got its hands around her throat. The pale, thin hands were Janie's hands, but they were much stronger than Janie's would ever be. Alys found that she had lost the sword. She tried to pry the hands away. The violet eyes were staring at a point just over her left shoulder. She balled her hand into a fist and raised it—and stopped. It was Janie's face, her sister's face.

Then she felt other hands pulling at the hands on her throat—the real Janie. The iron grip cutting off her air eased for an instant and she drew in a great, gasping breath. She took two handfuls of nightgown and twisted the creature around, banging it down hard against the wooden floor. The false Janie bucked and the real Janie flew across the room.

What followed was never clear in her memory. A chair was knocked over, the throw rug wound itself around her legs. It was a bare-handed fight: undignified, unsystematic, and deadly serious. Alys knew without question that the thing with Janie's face was trying to kill her.

And it was winning. It was stronger than she was, faster, tougher. It could outlast her. In one of her brief moments of advantage she threw it to the ground again, groping for something on the floor almost without knowing what she was doing. Her body was searching for something, telling her what to do, but her mind didn't catch up until she felt the sword in her hand.

Like the fight, the next few moments seemed much longer than they really were. The Janie-creature was pinned below her, eyes still wide and blank as it clawed and kicked. The sword was high in the air, but the feeling of life that had been there when she'd raised it in Morgana's house was missing. Still, it was a weapon.

She looked down at the Janie-thing. Then she looked across the room.

Janie herself had fallen back against a cabinet, sprawled, panting. Her face was as pale as the face of the nightgowned Janie on the floor, but her eyes met Alys's with intelligence and human understanding. She dragged in a deep breath and nodded, once.

Alys shut her eyes and raised the sword, which simply shook in her hands. She couldn't do it. A sob broke out of her throat and she started to pull back, to throw the sword away. Beneath her the sob was echoed by an animal snarl. Her eyes flew open and she found herself staring in shock at tawny fur and sharp teeth. With a gasp, she brought the point of the sword down with all her strength, pinning the bobcat to the floor.

Spitting, hissing, the creature tried to twist away, its golden eyes filled with fire and malevolence.

"Alys, hold on! Keep it there! Don't let go!"

She couldn't answer, but she dodged a murderous swipe of razor claws and gripped the sword hilt with both hands. Before her appalled gaze the tawny pelt of the bobcat melted and she was sitting astride a bucking, heaving dark mound. Black beavers from Mordor, she thought dizzily and tried to jam the sword in deeper. There was a low yowl which became a loud hiss. A forked tongue flickered out of a scaly lizard's face—a face with remarkably human blue eyes. The hiss became a thick bubbling noise and a tail smacked into the ground hard behind her. The sword was impaling a creature like a sea lion, whose muscles rippled under moist oily skin. Her grip on the hilt was slick with sweat.

The sea lion opened its mouth and roared and became something else. Alys didn't know what it was, and didn't want to know. Soft black hands flexed in the air as the thing gibbered and squealed.

I can't take much more of this, thought Alys. I wonder what happens if I do let go? She shut her eyes, clinging to the hope that the thing seemed to be getting weaker.

The shuddering beneath her stopped. The sounds stopped too. Cautiously she unsquinted and looked down, fingers still clasped trembling-tight around the sword.

It had turned into a giant frog-thing, with slack pebbled gray skin and bulbous, glazing yellow eyes. It was enormous, and smelled vile, but it was only moving feebly. It kicked once or twice and was still.

On shaky legs, leaning her weight on the sword, Alys pushed herself up and looked it in the face. It was beyond moving any more.

She let go of the sword and collapsed by it, her head in her hands. She ached all over. Janie crawled over from the cabinet until she was on the other side of the creature.

She looked up and met Janie's eyes across the frog. They were both breathing hard.

"Is it dead?"

"Yes. I—yes."

"Well," said Janie. She swallowed once or twice, and blinked, eyes wide with shock. She looked at Alys, then at the frog, and then back again. Then she said, rather blankly:

"You know, we don't do enough of these sister type things together."

Alys clapped a hand over her mouth to stiffle the giggles, but they burst out wildly. Janie began to giggle, herself, hysterically, and they rocked and shook on opposite sides of the froggy corpse. It had begun to disintegrate into a pile of gray slush, a fact which did not surprise Alys in the least. The smell was indescribable.

At last, gagging and choking, she wiped tears from her eyes, stumbled to her feet, and pulled her sword out of the mess. It took a good tug; the blade was imbedded in the floor. She wiped it on the throw rug in the corner.

Janie's giggles had died away to hiccups. She also got to her feet and stood looking down.

"What—what was it, anyway?" panted Alys.

"I'm still not sure," Janie replied unsteadily. "Not a boojum, though, and definitely not a phantasm. A shape changer of some sort, with seven incarnations. S'weird." She gave a shaky sigh and shook her head as if to clear the last remnants of mirth and hysteria.

Then, with an exclamation, she suddenly bent down and plucked something out of the pile of muck. To Alys it looked like a thick circlet of silver with curious designs inscribed on the surface. Janie examined it, rolling it between her fingers. Then, just as suddenly, she dropped it, almost flinging it away, wiping her fingers on her jeans.

"Alys, quick!" she cried. "As quick as you can, run and get Charles and Claudia down here. There isn't any time to lose. And we'll need other things—food and water—and a flashlight. *Hurry!*"

Her demeanor had undergone a complete change. Her words ran together, tumbling over each other, her purple eyes flashed with urgency. Alys stared at her, totally lost.

"I—what? What are you talking about? Where are you going?"

"To get a hammer. And a nail, and some string. And chalk, white chalk. And we'll need some blankets and things—anything you'd take into a fallout shelter. Go, go!"

Alys was still flummoxed. She stood where she was, frowning.

"We don't have a fallout shelter."

"I didn't say we did, I said those were the sort of things we need. Alys, don't just stand there! Run!"

"I want to know what's happening—"

"There isn't any *time.* It may be too late already!"

"To late for what? Janie, talk to me!"

"Will you please just do as I say?"

"Will you please just tell me what's going on!"

Janie's expression, as she stood frozen in her flight to the hardware closet, said she was being goaded beyond endurance. "If I told you that it is four hundred miles to San Francisco, and that a break in numinous rapport could be felt over twice that distance, and that Mach three is a limit only for corporeal entities, would that help? Does that make things any clearer? Oh, Alys, for once will you please just trust me!"

Alys wavered, bewildered and supremely frustrated. Abruptly she whirled and plunged up the stairs, seeing Janie turn back toward the closet the instant she obeyed.

She was able to take out some of her frustration on Charles. She rousted him out of bed by the simple expedient of yanking all his covers off and snapping on the light.

"Up! Now!"

"What're you doing? Leggo!" he shouted foggily, striking out.

"Get up and get downstairs fast, Charles. Bring your blanket and pillow. Hurry!"

She left him sitting bolt upright in bed, staring after her.

With her younger sister she was more gentle. Claudia woke at the first touch of Alys's hand on her shoulder, and sat up with wide eyes.

"Is it a fire?"

"No, but you've got to come quick. Bring your blanket and what you'll need for the night."

Claudia gathered up her blanket. She lifted a threadbare Paddington from the dresser, hesitated, then thrust it back, seizing her pillow instead.

Alys hustled her down the stairs. As they reached the bottom Charles appeared at the top, scowling, clad only in the bottom half of a pair of ancient seersucker pajamas. His hair was sticking straight up all over his head.

When he had descended far enough to see the dining room he slowed. His mouth dropped open. His eyes moved from the dining table, which had been pushed aside so Janie could hammer a tenpenny nail into the parquet floor, to the shambles of the room, to the puddle of evil-smelling sludge left by the frog-thing.

"Gee," he said at last, almost reverently. It was as if only this epithet, by its very mildness, could express what he felt when other words failed. "Gee whiz, Janie," he said again. "Is Mom ever going to be mad."

"Shut up and make yourself useful," snapped Janie, hammering her finger and sounding in that instant exactly like Morgana.

"Get the earthquake kit, Charles," said Alys, taking the hammer from Janie and driving the nail in with two swift, accurate blows. "And some food from the fridge."

"And something white I can pour. Granules. Not liquid." Janie had tied a piece of chalk to one end of a long string; now she tied the other end of the string to the nail and stretched it out taut. Using the string as a compass, her tongue between her teeth in concentration, she began to draw a circle on the floor with the chalk.

"I know what you're doing," said Charles, coming down the stairs with an air of dawning comprehension. "I saw it on TV. And what you need is salt."

"I don't care if it's salt or sand or flipping baby powder! It's just got to be white!" Janie had finished the circle and was now making eight marks at equal intervals around it.

Charles fetched a canister of salt while Alys shook Claudia's pillow out of its case and began tumbling cans from the shelves into this makeshift bag. At her instructions Claudia ran to get candles and matches.

"What else?" said Charles to Janie, who was carefully pouring a thin stream of salt over the perfect octagon she had drawn.

"Get all the stuff inside—and be careful! Don't break the lines."

"Charles may know what you're doing," Alys said, hanging grimly on to her patience as she slung supplies inside the circle, "but I don't. Why—"

"I'm pulling in the wards," Janie said shortly. "With less area to protect they should be much denser, much stronger. That's the theory, anyway. It's not something I ever expected to try with a virtue wand."

"Ah, the magic back-scratcher," said Charles.

Janie spoke without looking up. "You'd just better hope it works. Because as the wards are now, they don't stand a chance of holding up against—"

"Against *what?*"

"It's ready. Step inside quick! We've only got minutes, if that."

Alys bit back further questions and lifted Claudia over the salt line. "All right, we've got everything—no, wait!" She jumped back out and ran across the room.

Janie looked harried. "Alys, I'm not sure it's a good idea—"

"This sword stays with me! It was a good enough idea ten minutes ago!"

Charles glanced back and forth between his two sisters uneasily. "Given," he said, "the choice between the platinum-plus pigsticker and the magic back-scratcher—"

The sisters instantly joined forces in commanding him to

shut up. Alys plopped down cross-legged on the floor, pulling Claudia into her lap, dropping the sword by her side.

"Matches!" said Janie, holding out her hand and clearly dissociating herself from the whole sword question.

Charles slapped a pack in her hand. "Matches! But salt won't burn!" he added, just as crisply.

But this salt did, at the touch of a match. Janie crouched, black hair hanging in her eyes, to bury the tip of the rowan wand into one of the vertices she had marked. Low blue flames sprang up and flickered coldly. Claudia reached out tentatively to touch them and Alys snatched her hand back. Janie began breathing faster and a sheen of sweat appeared on her face. She shut her eyes.

The wand began to vibrate and Janie seemed to be having trouble holding on to it. The windows and sliding glass doors rattled suddenly, as if struck by a howling wind. Janie scooted back, still keeping the end of the wand in the flames, and reached straight up in the air with one hand. Her fingers crooked in a beckoning motion. Charles leaned back to give her room: it was rather crowded in the circle.

From everywhere, seemingly from the house itself, there rose a sound that was not really a sound. It was more a feeling of pressure that cut out all other noise. Over it, Janie was speaking words, no longer whispering but shouting, her head falling back. But as the spell rose to a crescendo her eyes focused on something beyond Alys and her voice turned shrill.

"Ensha'am—Irridiadore—*Charles, sit up! Alys, get him!*"

In backing away from Janie, Charles had come to the edge of the circle and was now sprawling with one hand outside it, supporting him. Alys seized her brother by the shoulder and pulled.

As he came flying toward her there was another non-sound: a deafening, slamming pressure. Every light in the house went out and a blast of wind shot straight upward, blowing Alys's hair toward the ceiling, drowning her scream. All around, where the circle of salt had burned with such flickering light, a painful violet brilliance erupted toward the sky.

And then there was silence.

Alys slowly lowered her hands from her ears. A fold of blanket had fallen across the salt line when she grabbed Charles. She picked it up and saw that the edge that had overlapped the circle was gone; cut as cleanly as if with a laser.

"This could have been your arm!" she shouted at Charles, waving the blanket in his face.

Janie, letting the virtue wand drop at last, slumped over with a sigh. Claudia said, "Ow," in a small voice and picked herself up off the sword.

Alys, too agitated to lecture Charles anymore, threw the blanket at him and looked around.

They were sitting in an octagonal cylinder of violet light. It was almost the blue color of the bottom of a gas flame. Yet it didn't look like flame, and not exactly like water, either, though it struck Alys as a bit like being in an upside-down waterfall. Because the waves of light were going upward, going *fast*, so fast they drew the eye with them, making it almost impossible to focus on anything outside. It made Alys's head reel to look at it.

It seemed to go right through the ceiling. Alys tore her gaze away and asked Janie, "How high?"

"Thirty leagues, I think. The top anchor point is well into the stratosphere anyway." Janie's voice was quenched. "It must have knocked the power out for blocks," she added.

Alys held a hand near the violet jet stream. She felt a faint rush of cool air against her fingers.

"It's all right to touch it from this side," said Janie. "But if anything from the other side tries—" She broke off, stiffening, peering through the circle. "Hang on, everybody. I think we're just about to get a firsthand demonstration."

Outside the Wards

A silence had descended over the house. It was hard to see out through the blue cylinder, but Alys could detect nothing moving. She realized she was holding her breath.

And then she saw it, a liquid flowing movement at the edge of her vision. It rippled almost like an eel, and it was easier to see, with her peripheral vision than when she looked at it directly. Claudia stirred in her lap and made a faint sound, pointing, and Alys caught a glimpse of another. Soon the darkened room was full of them, moving like whispers in a quiet church, rippling like silk.

One, soaring effortlessly like a gull riding an updraft, circled the cylinder, going round and round until it disappeared through the ceiling where the cylinder did. The wood and plaster did not deter it noticeably.

Another followed it, and another, and another. Soon the cylinder was encircled by them, following exactly in one another's path, spiraling upward.

"Now *those*," said Janie authoritatively, and with some satisfaction, "are boojums."

Charles looked at her. "Is this something I want to know?"

"They're sprites. Like—like elementals, sort of—"

"Oh, no." said Alys in protest. These ghostly fliers were

nothing like the elementals she remembered, the gentle guardians of the Wildworld marshlands. Even Elwyn's wild girls, the wood sprites, had at least looked human.

"Just sort of," said Janie. "Elementals are natural, they're born from the earth or the water or the woods. And they're usually benevolent—at least if there aren't any Quislais around to rile them. They watch over the land; they're part of the natural order.

"But boojums are *made.* Made by sorcery. And once you make 'em, you own 'em. They obey you. You can conjure them up from just about anything you like, but they fall into five basic classes: earth, air, fire, water, and illusion. Those things"—with a gesture outside the circle—"are air boojums."

Alys shuddered, hating the silky menace of them.

"I bet we'll see some other varieties as the night goes on," Janie added with a sort of gloomy relish. "Don't know what they'll do, though."

"Do you know where they *come* from?"

"Of course," Janie began scornfully, then she tensed, her attention caught by something outside the circle.

Alys caught her breath, squinting through the veil of blue light. She herself could see nothing, but she could *feel.* Tiny vibrations communicated themselves from the floor to her hand.

"Another quake?" Charles whispered.

Janie shook her head. "There. Watch."

The vibrations were stronger, and Alys fancied she heard a sound, like the rumble of far-distant thunder. The parquet floor outside the circle was rising, swelling; boards snapping and falling aside. The mound rose to a height of perhaps seven or eight feet, then it quivered and split at the top. A great clay-colored slug forced itself out of the crown, shaking off crumbs of earth. It began to hump its way down the dome. Others followed.

"Earth boojums," supplied Janie.

Outside, the wind screamed—and it really did scream, unless, as seemed more likely to Alys, it wasn't the wind at all. She peered through the eerie blue light to make out an eerie red light in the backyard. It seemed to rise and fall like the image of a flame.

She looked at Janie. "Fire boojums?"

Janie nodded, still looking half-appalled and half as if she would like to whip out a loose-leaf binder and start taking notes. "The backyard must be full of them—and who knows what else. I pity any stray cats out there tonight."

Alys and Charles agreed, and Claudia's feelings, of course, were in no doubt. But the next minute Claudia was clutching Alys by the arm, almost shrieking, too upset even to form a sentence.

"Alys!" she gasped out. "Benjamin Bunny! Benjamin Bunny! Oh, Alys, Benjamin Bunny!" She threw herself face-down in Alys's lap, sobbing hysterically.

The older Hodges-Bradleys exchanged dismayed glances. At last Charles, looking acutely uncomfortable, cleared his throat, and Alys knew without question that he was about to launch upon an explanation to Claudia about where the good bunnies go. Alys shook her head, forestalling him, then looked at Janie.

"Is there," she said, "any way out of this thing?"

Janie's expression snapped shut like a steel trap. "You," she said briefly, "are looped."

"Yes. Okay. But is there a way *out*?"

"No!"

"Think, Janie. How can you let me out and leave the three of you inside? Stop shaking your head at me. There must be a *theory*, anyway."

Janie stopped shaking her head and turned her back. Several minutes later she spoke coldly over her shoulder.

"I could take down an anchor point and make a rent in the wards. *Theoretically*, I ought to be able to hold it open for a little while, without the whole structure's collapsing."

"Good girl." Now that it came to it, Alys was not sure if she were glad or horrified that there was a way. Determinedly, she transferred Claudia to Charles, who was regarding her with wary disbelief, and, rising, she picked up the sword.

"Alys," said Janie, "you have always been bossy and a little weird. But just lately—and I really think you might want to think about this—"

"Just do it, will you?"

"—because Morgana is not going to be exactly overjoyed to hear that I violated the wards, overstepped my station, and risked all four of our *lives* for the sake of a barbecued bunny rabbit! Sorry, Claudia."

Alys rubbed the flat of the sword on her sleeve. The blue light flowed over it until she seemed to be holding a blade made of water. "Please hurry," she said softly.

Janie's sigh indicated that she had been pushed past the limits of human endurance. She began scanning various parts of the cylinder, all of which looked exactly the same to Alys. Finally she leaned forward and placed the virtue wand vertically against the wall. She muttered some words and slowly began to drag the top of the stick around, like turning a clock's hand from twelve to six. Behind the stick a clear space opened in the violet curtain; a half circle.

"One thing," she said with precision and between her teeth as Alys stepped forward. "This rent is not stable. I can keep it open for, maybe, a quarter of an hour, and then it shuts and it shuts for good. I do not have the power to do this again. *So you get back here in twelve minutes even if it means bunny brochette, okay?*"

"Okay," said Alys, a little shakily, and she stepped through the opening.

▼   ▼   ▼

The backyard had been transformed. It wasn't merely the strange illumination, red and orange and gold, which shone from all around like a thousand candles; familiar shapes had been masked and covered, distorted. Another of the large mounds stood in front of her, naked rock thrusting up through the grass, a broken sprinkler head dangling incongruously from its side. Transparent orange icicles hung from the eaves of the porch, trembling slightly and pulsing with light as she passed. Silky eels blanketed the patio furniture.

The clay-colored slugs gave way as she approached. One didn't move quickly enough and she prodded it with the sword; it hissed and withdrew. But when she glanced behind she saw that they were following, closing in. Above the flickering orange light the second story of the house loomed dark against the cloudy sky. She didn't know whether to be relieved or annoyed that the violet cylinder was spun out to the consistency of a fine mist above the roof. No one was going to report a UFO sighting or come to lend aid.

There was a black pool on the far side of the mound, between her and the rabbit hutch. To her cringing bare feet the water was cold, and the bottom seemed lined with smooth round pebbles. She was halfway across when she saw bubbles, a thin line like an electron trail in a cloud chamber, headed straight for her. She shied and stabbed at once, catching a glimpse of something streamlined and silvery that broke the water in an achingly lovely curve before it fell back from the sword. She didn't need Janie to tell her what it was.

Air, earth, fire, and water. She'd seen them all, now. There were slugs clinging to the sides of the rabbit hutch, icicles festooning the roof, and silkies on top. They pulsed quietly and seemed to be watching her, although they were all completely eyeless as far as she could tell.

She began dispatching them one by one, flipping the slugs off, slashing the trembling icicles, prodding the silkies into flight. It was almost too easy. She opened the cage door to see the white shape of Benjamin, rigid with terror but apparently still breathing.

She reached in and he shied away, gazing at her with fixed red eyes. When she took him by the skin at the back of the neck he struggled wildly for an instant, then went still. She tucked him under her free arm and started back.

Almost *too* easy. Although the slugs still followed her, almost on her heels, they stopped when she showed them the sword. A cautious triumph swelled in her. She was past the mound and in sight of the sliding door when she heard it.

"Ssssssss . . ."

Faint and dry as a dead leaf chased down the sidewalk by a brief wind. But she recognized it. Shocked, she turned.

The Feathered Serpents of the Wildworld were creatures of awesome power and majesty; vast, armored, almost indestructible. But not as babies. This serpent was only half a millenium old and still blue and coral instead of stark red and black. It was barely as long as her arm. She remembered the first time she had seen it, perishing from heat in a golden cage near the fire where Cadal Forge had put it. Then, it had barely been able to summon up the strength to talk to her. Now, nestled in the earth of a potted shrub, six pairs of wings limp and open instead of folded in a sleek ridge down its back, it seemed to have even less.

"Ssssssss . . ." The beadlike black eyes looked at hers pleadingly.

Hesitantly, she stepped toward it. How could it be here? Her serpent, which had been shut on the other side of the Passage when Morgana broke the mirrors.

But the Passage had opened again, if only for a second. And it had always loved her, always trusted her.

The black eyes shone dully in the red light.

"Sssssssss . . ."

Helplessly, she reached down to touch it.

Besieged

"It *worries* me," Charles was saying to Janie. "Do you understand what I mean? Not just right now. But everything lately—and sometimes she doesn't even seem like Alys anymore," he finished incoherently. "*Do* you know what I mean?" he demanded.

"All I know is she's only got five and a half minutes left," said Janie tensely, eyes on the grandfather clock in the corner.

A minute passed. Two.

"She's not going to make it," said Charles. He stood, looking pale in that eerie light. "Okay. Now."

"And fight them with what?" burst out Janie, understanding him perfectly. "Jujitsu? Tae kwon do? The *Force?*"

She was almost shrieking by the last words. Charles looked around the cylinder and picked up the canister of salt. He flapped a hand vaguely at her, in admonition or farewell, and climbed through the rent.

"Three minutes!" snarled Janie, sticking her head out after him. "Three minutes and I hope you both get fricasseed out there." If it hadn't been Janie he would have thought she was on the verge of tears.

▼ ▼ ▼

Alys was kneeling before the urn, the serpent wrapped around both her wrists. Except that it wasn't the serpent, of course, it was some wire-tough appendage of the creature, which had chosen for the moment to look like a potted plant.

"Stupid, *stupid,*" she told herself. Air, earth, fire, and water she had remembered. She had forgotten illusion.

The thing which had caught her wrists in a grip like steel cable under oilskin hadn't done anything to hurt her. It simply held her. But from all sides the others were closing in.

She kicked the closest slug away and felt a caress like chiffon on her shoulders. She shrugged violently, more offended by the silky eels than by any of the others. More than ten minutes have passed, she thought.

She felt another gentle touch on her back, on her arms, followed by a prickling like pins and needles. It wasn't painful. She made up her mind not to scream, and drew a breath. Then rough hands were tearing at her shoulders and neck and she heard cloth give way.

"Be quiet! Be quiet! I'm getting them off!" Charles shouted.

"Get the sword!" she shouted back, seizing precarious hold of herself. "Will you just get the sword and get me loose?"

He winced as he picked the sword up. The first awkward, overhand blow simply bounced off the blue and coral cable.

"Not there, you're going to cut off my hands! This whole thing is alive! Stab right in the middle, right down into the pot!"

He positioned the sword and leaned on it hard, driving the blade into ornamental gravel—or what looked like ornamental gravel. With a grunt he threw his weight on it and the sword sank deep. The serpent-cable whisked off Alys's wrists, giving her a first-class rope burn, and was snatched down inside.

She put her numb hands on his, which were damp and cold, and helped him wrench the sword out. Then she turned. Between them and the door was an army of slugs, layer on clay-colored layer. Eels drifted thick as smoke in the red air.

"They don't like salt—the slug ones," gasped Charles. "C'mon!"

Alys wanted to make a plan, to have Charles protect the rabbit while she went ahead with the sword. But what actually happened was that a phalanx of eels swooped in; she seized the rabbit by the loose skin on the back of its neck, and the next thing she knew she was pounding toward the house, with Charles brandishing the sword and yelling, "Run, Bambi, run!" madly in her ears.

The opening in the cylinder was no longer a half circle but a triangular wedge like a piece of pizza, and was rapidly getting thinner. She found Charles's dirty bare feet waving in her face as he dived through and then hands were reaching to take Benjamin and help her.

"Pull! Pull!" she shouted.

Her hips stuck. With one agonizing wriggle they came free and she went crashing down inside. Falling, of course, on Charles.

She scrambled up, promising herself to feel the bruises later. The virtue wand traversed the last few inches to twelve o'clock, knitting the wards up behind it.

Charles remained lying on his back, eyes shut. "Are we dead yet?" he inquired.

Alys looked at him wildly. His naked chest was streaked with enough mud to qualify him as an ancient Briton if only it had been blue instead of ochre, and his hair stuck straight up all over his head. Elwyn's witch mark gleamed faintly on his forehead.

She knelt beside him. He immediately opened one eye and hunched rapidly away without rising.

"No kissing! No kissing!"

"Okay. All right." She looked at Janie, who had collapsed in a tangle of black hair, and at Claudia, who was regarding her with precisely the same expression Benjamin had had when she first opened the hutch. She looked back at her brother. "Charles."

"Look," said Charles, sitting up at last, "will you just give the girl her rabbit?"

▾   ▾   ▾

When Charles and Claudia were asleep Janie and Alys sat and looked through the wall of coruscating blue. They spoke in low voices; there was a lull in the activity outside and stillness blanketed the house.

"I think it's time," said Alys, "to tell me exactly what's going on."

"I should've imagined that would be obvious," Janie whispered back. "We're beseiged. We're under sorcerous attack. By Thia Pendriel, I presume."

"Great reasoning, Mycroft. I'd gotten that far myself. But *why* are we under attack?"

"Because that frog-thing you killed, that shape shifter

with the seven incarnations, was hers. Her familiar."

"Like the vixen?"

Janie's lips drew back in distaste. "In a way. Some sorcerei don't keep a regular familiar, like Morgana keeps the vixen. Whenever they need one they pick up some nearby animal and use it. And when it's used up . . ." Janie shrugged and opened her hands expressively. "I figure she took some ordinary animal and changed it. Because that frog-thing was altered, it was *made* into a shape shifter, and made for one purpose: to get us. Even so, it must have taken a lot of work, and there was a bond between them. When it was killed she must have felt it. And I bet she was *furious!* When I realized that I figured the first thing she would do would be to send a gaggle of the nastiest boojums she could conjure up to teach us a lesson."

"But *why?*" Alys persisted. "Why send a familiar to harass us in the first place? We're nothing to her. Unless it's just spite—"

Janie gave a tired laugh. "Hardly. Alys, she's smart! She knows about us, knows how we know Morgana. And if she puts us in enough danger . . ."

Alys's stomach clenched. "She just might distract Morgana from whatever's going on up there."

"Bingo."

"Which means we've got to stick it out as long as we can, so that Morgana can get her business finished first."

"Yes. The problem is, I don't know how long we *can* stick it out. Ordinary boojums have a very short life span. But Thia Pendriel's got not only a Silver Staff but a Gem of

Power, and for all I know these things are planning to camp out until *next* Beltane."

Alys rested her head on her knees. They had food and water for a week, if that. Not to mention sanitary arrangements. "Janie," she said after a moment, "what are they, anyway? The Gems of Power?"

Janie gave her a narrow glance. "You shouldn't even know about them," she said. Then she shrugged. "All right, but you can't tell anybody else, okay?"

"Who," said Alys hollowly, "would believe me if I did tell?"

Janie grinned. "Right. Well, the Gems of Power are called the *bas imdril,* the Forgotten Gems, because they've been lost to the Wildworld for a long time. There were twelve once, but most of them disappeared ages ago. The Council has three in their stronghold at Weerien, but they're never used, never even touched."

"But what *are* they?"

Janie sighed and settled her chin on her knees. She put on her guest-speaker expression.

"A long time ago," she said, "there was the Golden Age of Findahl, all right? The dawn of the Wildworld. And in that time lived the greatest sorcerer the Wildworld has ever known."

"Darion—"

"—Beldar. Yes. Do you mind? Darion the Falcrister, he was called, the Nightweaver, creator of the Black Staff. He made it and it was more powerful than all the other staffs put together. So, guess what? He got to be King.

"Only he was a good guy, and so it worked out okay. The Wildworld was different itself, then. It was unspoiled and, and—*new,* sort of, and the sorcerei were only just discovering how to use magic wherever they found it. The councillors were good, and Darion was good, and everybody sang a lot, and learned a lot, and made things, and was happy. That's what they say.

"But it had to end, finally. Darion lived a long time, but at last he knew he was dying. And he realized that he couldn't just pass the Black Staff along to somebody else. It was too powerful. There was no one he could trust to wield it and not be corrupted.

"So he Unmade it. No one knows how. And what was left when he was done were Twelve Gems of Power, each containing a twelfth of the power of the original staff. That was when the Council of Twelve became the Ruling Council.

"But even the Gems were too strong, or else something had gone wrong when Darion Unmade the staff. A lot of people think that the Gems were changed or distorted when he did it, and that accounts for the weird things that happened afterward. Because weird things did happen to the councillors who held them. Three of them went mad and rebelled and tried to seize all the rest of the stones. And of course, the other councillors, the faithful ones, resisted.

"So there was a war. The Thousand Years' War. A lot of the Wildfolk were killed. Because in a sorcerous war *everybody* can participate. For a long time it looked like the rebels were going to win, and when they were finally conquered not one of the original faithful councillors was left alive, and all their Gems were lost. But there was peace at last.

"The new councillors—there were only nine from then on—tried to rebuild. But they never really had a chance. For one thing, they only had staffs to work with, because the three Gems that were left—the rebels' Gems—were locked away in the keeping of the Feathered Serpents. Nobody trusted anybody to touch them. And for another thing the Chaotic Zones had already started erupting. Suddenly there were Zones appearing all over and anybody caught inside them either died or went crazy. The Wildfolk had to abandon most of their old cities, and the little knowledge or art that had survived the war was destroyed in the Time of Chaos."

"The Chaotic Zones," murmured Alys, remembering the desolation she had seen left when the tide of Chaos in one receded for a while. It had turned a green marshland teeming with life into a desert of gray mud. And when the wild magic surged up again from its source it might do anything—from erecting a glacier to constructing crippled life out of the mud itself. The Chaos obeyed no law. Within its boundaries, all bets were off.

"That's the problem the sorcerei have been faced with ever since," said Janie. "Because every year there are more Chaotic Zones, and they get bigger. Everyone says they're worried about it, but so far nobody has come up with a practical solution."

"Cadal Forge had a solution," said Alys dryly, remembering.

"Taking *our* world. Yes. Well, in a way you can hardly blame him. We're just animals to the sorcerei. At least we're lucky that the Council thinks we're *wild* animals, and wants nothing to do with us. That's why Morgana's safe here even if Thia Pendriel does get the Passage back open. Because no matter how angry the Council is with Morgana over all the trouble she caused in the old days, they won't come into this world after her. It's their own law, and they'll keep it. Separation of humans and Wildfolk forever."

"What happens if Morgana goes back into the Wildworld?"

"Morgana," said Janie, "is not that dumb."

Alys chewed her lip meditatively. "How come Thia Pendriel hates her so much?"

"That," said Janie severely, "is gossip." After a moment she added, "Maybe because Thia Pendriel is a councillor, and the Council has been very down on Morgana these past five hundred years."

Alys snorted.

"All right. Because Thia Pendriel is a councillor, and a magistrate, and a flipping Silver Guildmistress, and she doesn't care beans about any of it. She wanted the Gold Staff when she was an apprentice and Morgana won it instead. Thia Pendriel was from one of the greatest houses in Findahl, and she *knew* she was better than any of the other contenders. But what she didn't know about was Morgana, who was half a human and half a Quislai and I bet Thia Pendriel doesn't know which she hates more. And ever since then Thia Pendriel has risen higher and higher in the politics of the Wildworld, but the one thing she always wanted she can never have."

"Uh," said Alys, remembering something. "So you think

she was serious when she said she'd fight Morgana alone, one-on-one, to win the staff honorably?"

"Who knows what goes on in her mind? But, yes, I think maybe she was serious, just for that moment. Just for that one instant she was willing to put away whatever other rotten plans she had, for the chance of gaining the Sun Gold honorably." Janie frowned a moment, then added reluctantly, "Anyway, there may be something else behind her feud with Morgana. I don't know any of the details, but the vixen let it slip once that there was some kind of cheating involved in the Competition when Morgana took the Gold."

"What kind of cheating? What do you mean?"

"I told you I don't know anything about it. I don't even know who was supposed to have cheated, and I'm not sure I believe the vixen anyway. She hasn't always been exactly truthful with us herself, you know."

Alys, who had not known this, or even suspected it, blinked and felt stupid. "Anyway," she said finally, retreating to safer ground, "we know that Thia Pendriel has got one of the lost Gems of Power and that she's willing to hurt us or even kill us to get Morgana off her back. And Morgana may or may not know about it. So where does that leave us?"

"Sitting in a purple pop bottle," said Janie shortly. There were shadows under her eyes and her face was puffy with tiredness. "Look, Alys, I don't know. Whatever Thia Pendriel is doing, Morgana thought it would be over by Beltane. Which is Sunday. Which means that *maybe* we can decant ourselves by then with some sanguinity of success."

"English, please."

Janie rubbed her temples. "I wonder," she said in a colorless voice, "if you have any idea how hard it is to always have to translate things into English-please. I said maybe we can come out then."

"Huh. Okay." Alys looked at her sister thoughtfully. "You'd better get some sleep."

Janie made some sort of protest, but since she could hardly keep her eyes open long enough to formulate a sentence, Alys won easily. When Janie was curled up beside the others Alys sat alone and gazed through the wards. She did not feel sleepy in the least; she needed to think.

Janie had explained everything—and nothing. Watching the play of light on the savagely transformed living room, Alys made a mental list of the questions that plagued her.

First of all, of course: what was Thia Pendriel doing? If one only knew that, the rest might be easy. But Janie, who was in the best position to know, refused even to speculate. And then there were the earthquakes, earthquakes which rocked the Passage. Thia Pendriel's work? If not, whose?

Too, Morgana had said that something had come through the Passage. It wasn't the bobcat or the soft black hands or the frog-creature; they were all manifestations of some ordinary animal that had been changed. It wasn't the boojums, which had been *made*, from the elements of earth. So, what? Something they had not even seen yet?

And then there was the rainbow. Alys's stomach tightened and a deeper feeling of unease flowed over her. The beauty and the wrongness of that sight disturbed her in a way she could not define.

Charles stirred in his sleep, muttering. Alys looked at him, sprawled unselfconsciously on his back, and at Janie curled almost into a ball, and at Claudia with the bunny beside her. She found herself looking at them appraisingly, almost as strangers, evaluating their strength and courage and endurance, although she had no idea what she was measuring them against.

She picked up the sword and gazed at it.

Charles stirred again, tossing and rubbing his arm in his sleep, and she felt a sharper flicker of concern. She watched him for some time until he settled down and slept quietly. And then she simply sat, while the violet jet stream flowed around her and the night wore itself away.

T W E L V E
▾ ▾ ▾
Journey North

The three younger Hodges-Bradleys woke stiff and cranky. Alys was stiff, too, but cautiously optimistic.

"I want you to look out the wards, Janie," she said. "You see? I haven't seen one of them for over an hour, not since it got light. Can you explain that?"

"Easy," said Charles, with a ghastly smile. "They had to go back to Transylvania to sleep."

"Shut up!" said Janie. She glared through the wards for half an hour before admitting there were no boojums in sight. Then she put her head down and clutched fistfuls of black hair in distraction. At last she looked up.

"Charles is right," she said, with an even ghastlier smile than he had given. "No, Alys, don't. I'm serious. There's only one possible solution: they're night runners. They only had so much power, probably enhanced by the moon, and they have to fly back up to get . . . recharged. It's not funny. As soon as it's dark again they'll be back."

"But for the time being we're free."

"No," said Janie. "Alys, I could probably take the entire octagon of wards down so we could get out. I *couldn't* put it back up. I'm a first-year apprentice, not a Guildmistress!"

Alys sighed. "Okay. So. What are our options?"

"As I see it, we have four. One, we can stay here inside the wards and hope to outwait the boojums. Two, we can drop the wards and head for the hills—literally. Like San Diego. Aunt Eleanore would put us up and there's at least a chance the boojums couldn't find us there. Three, I could collapse the wards completely."

"I thought you'd already done that."

"Not completely, no. The nested octagon is an intermediate state. But in an emergency it's possible to bring them right down on top of us—skintight, so to speak. We'd be knocked unconscious and stay that way until someone came to get us out, but we would be absolutely safe. We wouldn't even notice time passing."

"All right," said Alys. "What about number four?"

"Four . . . well, four, we could summon Morgana."

Charles and Claudia brightened at the very mention of this, but Alys simply looked expressionlessly at the heavy twisted bracelet on Janie's wrist.

"And she would really come? Morgana? She'd let Thia Pendriel get away with whatever she's trying to get away with just to come rescue us?"

Janie's voice was equally expressionless. "She'd come."

There was a silence. Charles scratched his collarbone and looked hopefully at the ordinary pale daylight coming in the sliding glass door. Claudia cuddled the bunny and rocked a little. Janie sat and stared at Alys, and Alys sat and stared at the sword. It threw back dazzling flecks of light, like the swarming sparks in Morgana's staff, only blue-violet instead of gold. The light nudged at her memory, stirring things which would not come to the surface.

She wasn't aware she'd been holding her breath until she let it out.

"Well," she said. She took the sword and her palm tingled with warmth. "I've got another idea." She hefted the blade and met two pairs of trusting blue eyes and one pair of wary purple. "I want to go north and help Morgana."

It took a moment for this to sink in. "Round the bend," said Janie flatly when it finally had. "Bats in the belfry, but nobody's home."

"Yes. Still."

Charles, looking a good deal more awake than he had a few minutes ago, exchanged a glance with Janie. "Morgana," he said, speaking slowly and carefully as if to a lunatic of great strength and unknown temperament, "does not need help, Alys. *We* are the ones who need help. And some of us need it more than others," he added under his breath.

"I know," admitted Alys. "It doesn't make sense . . . but somehow I feel that she needs us. In my dreams . . ." She broke off and hefted the sword again.

Charles and Janie exchanged another glance during which each tried to hand the problem over to the other. At last Janie spoke.

"Just what is it you propose to do? You wouldn't even know how to find Morgana."

"No, but you would, wouldn't you? Of course, once we find her she may send us home for all I know. But it's better than sitting here waiting for those things to come back, and it's better than running and hiding. I don't want to run and hide anymore. I want to fight."

"I see," said Janie crisply, her eyes purple slits. "The

coward dies a thousand deaths, the hero dies but one, eh? The boy stood on the burning deck and all."

Alys flushed, but shrugged. She did not relinquish her grip on the sword.

Janie, after another moment of fierce silence, suddenly snorted and rested her forehead on her hunched-up knees. "Right-ho. When do we start, boss?" she muttered.

"*What?*" said Charles.

Claudia looked up from the bunny to Alys, her face stern. "Where am I going to be," she said, "while you're doing all this fighting?"

"With us," said Alys promptly and unemotionally. "You can talk to animals. We need you."

Claudia nodded, once. Charles looked from her to Janie in disbelief.

"Both of you. I thought *you* had better sense, Claude. Janie just wants the chance to do more magic, because she's so *good* at it. She doesn't care what happens to the rest of us, as long as she can write it up. And Alys has gone off the Orange Plunge. But you."

"You don't have to come," said Alys quietly.

"That," said Charles, bitterly, "is where you're so wrong. Good ol' Charles always comes." He stood up, and, because there was no place to go, turned his back on them.

Janie looked at Alys, then stood, herself. "Charles," she said. She and her twin, however dissimilar in appearance, were precisely the same height, and when he turned back she was looking him directly in the eyes. "We need you," she said. "And not just to 'come along.'"

Charles stood quite still a moment, then nodded stiffly.

Alys stared at each of the twins in wonder, and even Claudia looked as if she were suddenly confronted with a pop spelling quiz on a list of words she'd never seen. It was as uncharacteristic for Charles to be seriously angry as it was for Janie to show this frightening maturity.

"There is a minor technical problem," said Janie, sitting calmly down again. "You said I would be able to locate Morgana, Alys. And that's true—as long as I steal some things I shouldn't even lay hands on and have a familiar to help me focus. The stealing I can deal with, that's about par for the course. But the familiar isn't so easy." She made a great point of not looking at the Ace bandage around her thumb.

"The vixen . . ." Charles began, then stopped as Alys shook her head at him. His gaze shifted apologetically to Claudia. It lingered there, and the slightest shadow of a bemused grin appeared on his face. Claudia, chin on bunny, frowned back. Alys looked at Charles in puzzlement, then at Claudia, and then she felt the corner of her own mouth twitch.

Janie glared at them. "Oh. No. Absolutely not."

Charles began to chuckle. Alys bit her lips.

"I *won't*," said Janie. "You don't understand, I'd be responsible for it for *life*. I won't do it, I tell you."

Claudia, after looking at the other two, beamed suddenly with understanding. "He's very smart."

"He's a *rabbit*," said Janie. "I'd never live it down."

"You can't make an omelet without breaking eggs," said Alys serenely. "Pride goeth before a fall."

"I'll bet he won't even do it. Rabbits are scared of every-thing—"

Claudia bristled, then looked at Benjamin with sudden doubt. She bent to whisper into the white ear.

"He *will* do it," she said, raising her head after a minute. "He is scared, but he will."

"That's it," said Charles encouragingly to Benjamin. "Be a devil."

"I will get you for this," said Janie to Charles, "if it's the last thing I ever do."

▾ ▾ ▾

The wards were down. Outside, the clouds began to thin out and scatter, but it was still gray and chilly as Janie pedaled back from Morgana's house with a backpack filled with sorcerous instruments.

Alys, Charles, and Claudia had packed a sort of picnic lunch comprising most of the earthquake kit supplies and all the granola bars they could find. The house looked, as Charles pointed out, even worse in the daylight than it had at night. There was little they could do to straighten it up or minimize the damage. When Janie arrived they gathered their provisions and tramped outside.

"Oh, God," said Alys, striking a palm to her forehead as they stepped onto the driveway. She had forgotten. They would have to drive the Swinger.

They all looked at it, gloomily, except for Janie, who suddenly grinned.

The Swinger was a standing joke among Alys's classmates at the high school. Her parents owned two other cars: a

Jaguar, which was always at the shop waiting for the arrival of obscure British parts, and a station wagon, which was presently at the airport. Her father had bought the Swinger because it was cheap, and big, and wouldn't take much harm from any scratches a beginning driver might add. The problem was Alys scarcely dared to drive it. It tended to change gears of its own volition and the brakes either jammed or wouldn't work at all. Her father said there was nothing physically wrong with it, but Alys noticed he wouldn't drive it either.

Opening the garage door revealed it in all its splendor, flamingo pink where it was not primer green; and Alys felt a familiar sinking at heart. Every encounter with the Swinger was a battle.

And today it was in one of its more cantankerous moods. The engine refused to turn over, and when it finally did, it flooded. When Alys tried to release the emergency brake it stuck. When it unstuck the steering wheel locked. After several minutes of swearing and wrestling the wheel moved, but the oil and the alternator lights went on. At last, on the corner of Center Street and Taft Avenue, there was a sound of rending metal and the Swinger abruptly shut down altogether.

"That's *it,*" said Alys, dealing the front tire a vicious kick as she walked around to put up the hood. "This is the last straw. It's nothing short of suicide to go out in this thing."

She and Charles had both taken auto shop, but had long ago realized that the inner workings of the Swinger bore absolutely no resemblance to anything they'd seen there. It was far too ancient.

"What we need," Charles said in feeling tones, "is a hot bran mash to feed it."

"What we need," said Alys bitterly, "is an exorcist."

Despite all their proddings and reconnectings, the engine remained uncooperative. The afternoon wore on, and overhead the clouds parted to allow the sun to shine bravely on them. Above the smell of wet concrete and raw gas rose the smell of hot metal and singed rubber.

"Having a little problem there?"

Alys, behind the wheel listening to Charles yell "Try it now," looked up. It was Bliss Bascomb, with her older brother Brent. In a convertible. A red convertible. A Beamer.

Brent Bascomb looked a lot like his sister. He had the same one-sided smile, the same fine, light hair, the same year-round tan. Alys looked over the hood at Charles, who, if he had washed since last night had not washed much, and at Claudia sitting in the backseat clutching the rabbit, and at Janie beside her. Janie was looking ahead, expressionless, hands folded tightly in her lap.

"Did you run out of gas? Or does that thing run on rabbit pellets?" giggled Brent. Alys looked at him with fascinated disgust. It was bad enough when girls giggled. Janie went strawberry-colored, but didn't move. Alys looked at her, then back at Brent.

"No offense," he said, turning his own engine off and climbing out to stand beside Alys's door. "I bet I can give you a hand—maybe even two. Hey, what's that on the seat? Your kid brother's sword?"

He gave Charles a brilliant comradely smile. Charles stared back, his mouth slightly open. Alys looked at Janie again, then back at Brent, then at the brand-new Beamer, and then she fixed her own eyes straight ahead.

"Right," she said distinctly to Janie. "Do it."

Janie's hands unclasped, then reclasped tremulously in her lap. She shut her eyes for a moment and sank down in her seat, a beatific smile lighting her face. Then she straightened back up.

"Come over here, Brent," she murmured huskily, her purple eyes dilated and dreamy. "I've got something I want you to smell."

▾ ▾ ▾

"I thought you said stealing you didn't have a problem with," said Charles.

"It's just more fair this way," said Janie, shutting the passenger door of the Swinger gently on her classmate. "Like an exchange, see? You understand, don't you, Bliss?"

"Oh, yes," said Bliss sincerely. She did, in fact, understand. After one deep breath of crushed Worldleaf she and her brother understood more about the Wildworld than any other mortal beings on the planet—except the four who had just explained it to them. The virtue of Worldleaf was that it enabled the listener to perceive the truth in its purest form, sweeping the mind free of the clouds of old prejudice or misapprehension. And the truth was that the Hodges-Bradleys needed the convertible more than the Bascombs did. No reasonable being could deny that. The Swinger was payment in kind, if not in quality, as Janie pointed out.

"They understand *now,*" agreed Charles pointedly. "But what happens in a little while when the effects wear off and they remember everything except the reasons why they did it? They're going to be telling their parents they gave their car away to some kids who made them smell a leaf. And what do they say *then?*"

"They'll make up some reasonable explanation, the way the police did last year for not arresting us," said Janie crossly. "They'll fill in the blanks in their memory with something that makes sense to them."

"What *I'm* worried about is that's just about the last of the Worldleaf," said Alys, peering at the single tiny sprig left in the baggie. "I didn't tell you to use *that* on them."

"I suppose you'd rather I said three magic words and changed them both into ring-tailed lemurs," shouted Janie furiously, snatching the plastic bag back. "Shazam! Ka-blooey! Morrow Krinkle Frazetta!" She made arcane stabbing motions at the Bascombs with stiff fingers.

"All right," said Alys, herding her into the Beamer. It was something of a comfort to have the old unreasonable Janie back again, even if she did go on shouting invocations all the way down the street. Bliss and Brent waved good-bye rather vaguely, from the front seat of the Swinger, until they were out of sight.

▾ ▾ ▾

THIRTEEN

The Wild Hunt

It had turned into the perfect afternoon for riding in a convertible. Alys's straight fair hair flew back in the wind and Janie's wild black tangles grew wilder and more tangled. Charles, who was directly behind her, kept spitting bits of hair out as he grinned from side to side at everyone on the freeway. The only one who wasn't enjoying it was Benjamin. He trembled and stared wildly, pink nose quivering. Claudia stroked him and whispered to him, but it didn't seem to help much.

"North *where?*" Alys shouted to Janie over a wind that roared like a vacuum cleaner.

"Just north for now," Janie shouted back, the road map flapping in her face. "Stay on Highway 5 until we get through Los Angeles. Then we'll reconnoiter."

Reconnoitering consisted of lunch, some odd manipulations with the shivering Benjamin, and the production, finally, of a round beveled shaving mirror which Janie held flat in her lap. It was not one of Morgana's magical mirrors; they had all been broken last year at the winter solstice. It was just a good reflective surface for a visioning circle.

"He says he thinks he feels something, but he's not sure," reported Claudia after conferring with the rabbit. "He's nervous. And—well, he's not as smart as I thought," she added in a low voice to the others, wincing. "He doesn't have words for a lot of things."

"Might as well have used a chicken," muttered Janie. "But he does sense something almost due west of here?" she added aloud, ignoring Claudia's glare. "That's what I'm getting. It's far away—seventy miles or eighty miles at least, right around Santa Barbara. But it's a definite hot spot." Her breath clouded the already cloudy surface of the mirror, where a livid green blob sat in a spider web of pale lines on a coppery background.

"Yes," said Claudia stiffly. "He says it feels like magic."

"But whose magic?" said Alys. "I got the impression that Morgana was going farther north than that. Can we be sure it's her?"

Janie sighed as the visioning circle cleared. "Not with this," she said. "I'm much too far away to get a fix. Even close in, I probably couldn't hook into it without first knowing what it was. The circle's not meant for spying; it's for personal communication between friends."

"Thia Pendriel showed us pictures of Alys and Charles in the fountain behind Fell Andred," Claudia pointed out.

"Yes, and Thia Pendriel's lifestudy has been bringing far-distant scenes to light. In other words, she's a master at it; not just visioning circles but spheres and camera obscura in general." Janie's voice trailed off and she looked thoughtful. "I wonder . . ." she said. "Do you know, I almost think I could do it."

"Do what?"

"Use the visioning sphere. I've never done it before, but I know the theory." With sudden animation she dived into the backpack.

"You brought *that?*" said Alys, drawing back in exactly the same way she had when Claudia had casually pulled a king snake out of her lunch box one morning at breakfast. "*Why?*" The last time she had seen that nest of wires it had been supporting a glowing green sphere, with a face in it. . . . An instant's memory flicked across her consciousness and she saw the face again, then it was gone. "That thing is dangerous," she said finally, recovering herself. Though she could not explain it, she felt the conviction of her words.

"It's powerful," said Janie mildly. "But I think I can handle it. Of course, if that hot spot turns out to be Thia Pendriel instead of Morgana, she might detect us through the sphere. But I think it's worth the risk."

"And I think it's *not.* Not when we can cut over west and take Highway 101 to Santa Barbara. Then we can see for ourselves. If the hot spot is Morgana there must be a safer way to communicate with her. And if it's Thia Pendriel we can get away before she knows we're around."

Janie shook her head impatiently. Her eyes were still blazing violet. "But this will save us time. If I use it and discover that it's not Morgana, that it's something dangerous—"

"—then we may have told something dangerous exactly where we are." Alys knew some of her fear of the visioning sphere might be irrational, but she didn't care. She hated the thing. She cut off Janie's Madame Curie look with a glare. "I am not going to sacrifice the four of us just because enquiring minds want to know, Janie. This is not an experimental condition."

"But—"

"No!"

Charles and Claudia looked at each other resignedly and each took another sandwich. They were used to sitting on the sidelines during endless domestic debates. But now Janie, instead of arguing, plunged her hand into the backpack again, drawing out a small shiny globe with something green and fluttering inside. She stood and placed the nest of wires on a rock.

"Janie, put that down."

Janie set the little globe above the wires, where it bobbed like an egg in water, not quite touching them.

"Janie, I mean it. *Now!*"

Janie ignored this. She rubbed Benjamin's fur briskly before Claudia could snatch him away, causing it to stand on end. With her other hand she took the virtue wand and held it to the wire nest.

"You asked for it!" said Alys. She grabbed Janie by the windbreaker. Janie shook herself free and put out a furious hand to steady the wire nest. Alys spun her neatly around by the arm and punched her in the stomach.

The air came out of Janie's lungs in a surprised grunt. She sat down hard and stayed there, looking at up at Alys stupidly.

Charles and Claudia were looking, too, frozen in midbite. They had never in their lives seen Alys hit anybody.

Breathing hard, she stared back at each of them in turn, Janie last. "All right," she said, her throat sounding clogged. "Get up. We've got to drive."

Janie simply sat looking at her almost blankly. Her hand was still wrapped around the virtue wand, and for a moment Alys felt a shudder down her backbone, as if *her* fur had been rubbed the wrong way. Janie held her gaze for another minute; then, so deliberately that it was a purposeful act, looked away and began to gather up the sorcerous implements which had scattered. In silence the others followed her lead. Charles helped her up and opened the door for her, then sat down beside her in the backseat. Claudia, who had been clamoring to sit up front, climbed in with the rabbit pressed to her chest. She did not look at Alys. Neither did the others.

Face feeling stiff and sore, Alys got behind the wheel and began to drive west. The sword, which she had placed crosswise between the front seats, bumped her knee gently.

▼　▼　▼

Alys had never known what it was like to have all three of the others against her. She thought, as she stared sightlessly through the windshield, steering automatically and much more competently than she ever had during driver's ed class, that Janie must have had this feeling often, especially in the old days. She wondered how she had stood it.

The coastal highway to Santa Barbara would have been scenic, but a low fog was flowing down between the hills like the vapors from dry ice. Through the fog shone the setting sun, creating a strange halo of enormous diameter around itself.

At last Alys got off on a narrow side road which commanded a reasonable view of the towns of Goleta and Santa Barbara below. Alys had been here once before, visiting a cousin at the University of California there. It looked different now, isolated points of light in a sea of mist. She took a deep breath.

"Janie. Can you do something with that mirror to give us a general idea where to go? Something even Thia Pendriel, if it is Thia Pendriel, can't possibly tap in on?"

There was a pause. When Janie replied it was in as cold a voice as Alys had ever heard. "I can try. Is that what you want?"

It was, only she wanted Janie to argue and explain and suggest ideas instead of receiving her orders like a junior officer. She nodded jerkily.

She heard the whisper of a backpack zipper and the resonant ring of glass. Claudia leaned over the backseat to contribute the bunny.

"Don't pull his ears," she whispered. "He doesn't like it when you pull his ears."

Alys sat and gazed into the sun. Through the fog it shone as dull a red as Cadal Forge's Red Staff. Around it the halo looked as fixed and immovable as the rings around Saturn.

"It's near dark," said Janie from behind her. "And I'm not at all sure what I'm picking up. It's not a single point, it's a diffuse cluster of sorcerous power scattered around the campus itself."

"Could Morgana be part of it?"

"Possibly," said Janie with deadly quiet.

"We'd better go see, then." Without waiting for discussion from the others, she put the car in gear.

Her head was throbbing by the time she cruised onto the campus, paying a parking fee to drive onto a snaky road that dead-ended against a lake. To her right faint lights shone in the windows of a series of low-slung buildings. To her left was the ocean.

"So where is it?" she said, knowing perfectly well that she sounded belligerent. She felt belligerent.

"You're sitting in the middle of it," said Janie in deliberately level tones. "There are hot spots all around you. A very big one at three o'clock."

Three o'clock was in the midst of the low buildings. Alys swiveled around to address the two in the backseat. "I'm going to try to get a look at whatever it is," she said. "You will all stay here."

"Wrong," said Charles. "I mutiny."

"Shut up," said Janie to Charles.

"*What?*"

Janie glared at him. "Someone's got to be in charge, you idiot. *You* certainly can't do it, so she might as well. You're only making more trouble."

Charles got out of the car by the simple expedient of slamming a hand on the door and vaulting over. "You two *deserve* each other," he shouted. "And I am hitching a ride home!" He stalked away, due east.

Claudia sat gulping and rocking Benjamin. She began to snivel.

"Oh, stop it!" said Alys in a suppressed scream. "All right. All right. I'll go after him."

"And what," said Janie, in a terrifying voice, "do you expect us to do while you're doing it?"

"Stay here," Alys said with a kind of choked hysteria.

They stared at each other, eyelash to eyelash, a long moment. Then Janie pulled back and nodded compliance.

Claudia watched Alys's tawny head as it moved away between the buildings by the lake, then turned to look at Janie, who was staring into the mist as if she could bore holes in it. Her nerve crumbled. A great wail rose in her chest.

"I want to go *home,*" she bawled, flinging the door open and stumbling down the path after Alys.

Janie swore, softly but decisively, and followed.

▼   ▼   ▼

Charles had reached the first of the low-slung buildings as the mist closed in. It floated over the lake like dragon's breath and combined with the twilight to twist ordinary shapes into fantastic edifices. He had to order his feet to come to a stop before he could pull up. What was he doing, anyway? Sure, Alys was being unbearably bossy, but Alys was always unbearably bossy. Just as Janie was always doing six impossible things when you least expected them. Exasperating, but nothing to lose your head over.

And now. Mist and trees. Woods, almost. Everywhere. He turned in his tracks, with a terrible feeling of déjà vu. The last time he had been alone in a misty, twilit forest . . .

A shape reared out of the mist behind him and he almost yelled. It was a wild girl, all right, but not the kind with budding horns and eyes that threw moonlight back at you. It was Alys.

All his former truculence returned in a second. "Go on! Want to hit *me*, too? Take your best shot!" He crouched.

"Oh, have you gone crazy?" she said, seizing him by the elbows and shaking him. He aimed a punch at her and she fended it off easily with her forearm. "Stop it, blast it, or I *will* hit you! Are you *nuts?*"

He tried to jerk away from her. "Let go of me or you'll see just how nuts!" he shouted, utterly reckless of the consequences. They wrestled briefly and unproductively. Charles got a hand free and was just about to see if he really did know what a right hook was when something sailed over their heads.

Both their breaths came out in a whistle and they froze, locked together and staring. The something landed in front of them and turned swiftly and they saw it was a stag. A ten-point buck if I've ever seen one, thought Charles dazedly. A man was on its back.

There were other animals around them, in the mist. Some were more or less like horses; most weren't. All had riders clad in a silver-green almost the exact color of young birch leaves. At their feet lean hounds crouched, looking eager.

A strangled sound from the path directly to their rear heralded the presence of Janie and Claudia. They were clinging together, exactly, Charles observed, as he and Alys were now doing.

The man on the stag gave a slight tilt of his head and animals surged up around the two lagging girls, herding the four children together. The man's pale face was beautiful and utterly remote, and silver light reflected from his eyes. Far off, a hunting horn sounded, not two or three notes but up and down a whole scale of melody. It was the loveliest and most chilling sound the human children had ever heard. It awakened in them a primal instinct to run.

"No, *don't*," gasped Janie, clutching at Charles's arm. "Whatever you do, for pity's sake, don't run. It's the Wild Hunt."

Charles painfully unclenched a handful of Alys's sweater. "What do we do, then?" he said, getting out each word separately.

"Walk," said Janie. Her own voice was shaking and she took a moment, visibly, to compose herself. "Just—walk. Don't look at them. Just—slowly—walk away."

"I'll go first." Alys spoke in a bare breath of a whisper, but her voice was steady.

"No! Charles goes first. Don't argue."

Charles did not really want to know why. He began to shuffle down the path, eyes averted from the shining figures all around, his sisters moving in a huddle behind him. The horses-or-whatever shied and pranced as he went by, and the dogs bared their teeth, but all let him pass. He could feel pale eyes on him, waiting for him to break and run.

Sweat was running down his forehead by the time they cleared the trees. Distantly, he could hear shouting and shrieking, and also musical cries that came from no human throat. As he stepped off the gravel path onto concrete he saw what he first assumed were swoon spots before his eyes.

He blinked and the spots remained. Pale green moths, circling beneath a street lamp. And at the foot of the lamp was a slim figure clad in white, talking to a man sitting on the ground.

Charles was already going in that direction, and he was not at all sure the ghostly riders would let him diverge anyway, so he kept on walking until he drew abreast of the pair. The seated man wore wire-rimmed glasses and a dazed expression. The slim girl was Elwyn.

She was wearing an oversized T-shirt which hung almost to her knees, and that was all she was wearing, unless you counted the little bell around her ankle. Her hair flooded in a tide of impossible radiance down her back, and her eyes were blue as gems in her delicate face. Charles's tongue stuck to the roof of his mouth.

"And we do dance so beneath the stars," Elwyn was saying in a candid, conversational tone to the seated man, absolutely oblivious to the rest of them. "In a fairy ring, by moon at midnight." The man, who looked irresistibly like an ancient-history professor, nodded slowly as if he found this unsurprising. "Of course, we then cast off all our clothes," Elwyn continued, "and run wild among fires in the woodland. Shall I show you how we do *that*?"

The man in the wire-rimmed glasses looked intensely wistful. "No," he said, after a moment, with an apologetic glance at the four mortal children behind Elwyn. He took off his glasses and began to polish them, clearing his throat in a dazed sort of way.

Alys, who had never got along with Elwyn Silverhair, jabbed Charles hard in the shoulder blade. "Say something!"

Charles looked at her, then at the straggly-moustached

man, who smiled faintly at him as if he were a brother, and finally at Elwyn. He cleared his own throat.

"Uh," he said. "Hello."

The girl with hair like moonlight and starlight turned to him blankly. The scholarly man put his glasses back on over somewhat watery blue eyes, and stood. "Good-bye, my dear," he said. "Thank you for showing me your dance. I'll never forget it. I—I live with my mother, you see." And he walked slowly back the way the Hodges-Bradleys had come, blinking bemusedly, not seeming to see the riders on either side of him.

Charles spared him one look. "So do I," he muttered. "So what?" Alys poked him again.

Elwyn, however, had lost interest. She swatted at one of the pale green moths absently and turned away, her anklet jingling.

The voice of the white-haired man on the stag rose from behind them. "Fair game, oh my mistress?"

"*No,*" hissed Janie to Charles just as Elwyn turned and said, "Yes," in tones of completely nonmalicious indifference.

Something went *whoosh* beside his foot and Charles, staring at it, recognized a highly ornamented but perfectly serviceable spear. He flung back his head and gaped at the white man.

The gesture seemed to arrest the rider. "This one hath a Mark," he commented, in the sort of voice Charles's mother might use to say, "this melon has a soft spot."

Elwyn was still devoting most of her attention to slapping the moths which circled her adoringly. But Charles did not need the jabbing of Alys and Janie in order to catch on. He took a step toward her and was arrested only by two more spears, one from either side, that crossed in front of him as he frantically pushed the hair back off his forehead.

"Elwyn! Look! It's me! Remember?"

Elwyn clearly didn't. She regarded him with absent repudiation. One of the nonhorses whickered impatiently.

"Come on, you've got to remember. You kissed me. Here. See?"

Elwyn was shaking her head, diverted but not convinced. Suddenly she bent forward and looked at the mark on his forehead. She reached one tapered finger to touch it and laughed with glee.

"I *do* remember. Why, you're the Charles boy!"

"That's right," said Charles, holding up his empty hands and turning as he said it to make sure all the riders heard. "The Charles boy, that's me, all right."

A spear was plucked out of the ground on either side of him. The white man leaped gracefully off the stag to retrieve the last one; he bent the knee to Charles briefly before leaping back on. Most of the riders followed as he rode away, taking the five-foot hedge as if it were a mere twig in the road. Charles felt a shaky breath hiss out of him and stared after them.

"There," said Janie, sounding somewhat tremulous herself. "I told you. Beasts of air and field and water; certain sprites and elementals—"

"I remember all of you," put in Elwyn, in self-congratulatory tones. "You," she said to Alys, "hurt my head."

"You already forgave her for that," said Charles. Now

that his initial relief was over what he felt was the all-too-familiar sinking feeling of trying to engage in rational conversation with Elwyn. "Remember?"

"Oh, yes," said Elwyn vaguely, clearly not remembering but willing to take his word for it. "And you and I danced in the moonlight and counted stars till the dawn," she added, warming.

"No," said Charles. "We *talked* about doing that. *You* talked about it. But we didn't."

"We didn't?" said Elwyn, genuinely surprised.

"No!" There was only so much he could bear, even to save his sisters' lives.

"Well, then, we must do so now," Elwyn said brightly and whistled. It was a bird trill, but what came in answer was some magnificently antlered animal heavier of bone than the stag, with a shaggy-furred neck. An elk, maybe. In one fluid motion she leaped upon its back; and gracefully, effortlessly, she caught Charles up by the arm in front of her. With another trill, but without a backward glance at the three females left gaping, she disappeared into the night.

F O U R T E E N
▼ ▼ ▼

A Savage Place

"I was wrong," said Janie in an utterly detached voice, looking at the place where Charles had been, "when I counted three hot spots of magic already in this world. I remembered Morgana, Thia Pendriel, and us. I forgot about Elwyn."

"And those—things?" said Alys. "They're what Morgana sensed coming through the Passage?"

Janie nodded. "It's the Wild Hunt. They're wood elementals. It's sport to them."

Claudia made a faint sound. "But what about Charles?" she demanded. "What do we do?"

"We do nothing," said Janie quietly. "There's nothing we *can* do. He's riding the Wild Hunt with a Quislai. Not even the Weerul Council could stop that. The councillors are as scared of them as anybody."

"But Elwyn won't *hurt* him?" Claudia quavered.

"No," said Janie, communicating the qualifier silently to Alys alone. Elwyn might not hurt him deliberately, but it was at least even money that she would drop him, or forget him in some inconvenient place, or absentmindedly lead him into a Chaotic Zone if she could find one. Alys shut her eyes and turned away, taking her self-control in both hands.

"Back to the car," she said thickly.

The noise of the hunt got fainter and fainter as they went,

intermingled with yelling and the distant crash of glass.

Alys couldn't help but ask it. "What do they do with the people who do run from them?"

A muscle twitched in Janie's jaw. "Run them till they drop," she said. "The stories don't agree about what happens if they catch you. I only know that sorcerei get out of the way *fast* if they hear the *Fava-se-rá*—that's the opening bars of the hunting call." She gave the strange syllables an even stranger intonation, very staccato and dissonant, rising in both tone and volume. The fine hairs erected on the back of Alys's neck. Those four notes spoke to some part of her brain that was afraid of giant lizards and which wanted to scurry up a tree or burrow underground for safety.

"Janie . . . Morgana never rode with them, did she?"

"I hardly think this is the time," said Janie, but of course that answered Alys's question perfectly clearly. They got into the car and drove.

But they were driving blind now. The visioning circle remained empty, or at least empty of anything but the writhing reddish shapes that Janie called background noise. It was Janie who said it at last.

"Alys, it's over. We've got nothing to go on. Morgana said north, but that could mean anywhere from here to Anchorage. A needle in a haystack is nothing in comparison. We tried."

"No," said Alys harshly.

"Alys, face facts."

Alys clenched her teeth to keep from yelling at Janie. But the falling feeling in her stomach and the ache in her throat told her what she knew inside. Janie was right.

She took the next off ramp, turned around, and started back toward home. It was going to be hard to stay awake during the rest of the drive. She rolled down the window and switched on the radio.

". . . at eleven twenty-eight a temblor measuring four point five on the Richter scale," the resonant voice of the DJ said. "No injuries have been reported, but power lines are out all over the northern Bay Area. PG and E says three thousand homes will be without electricity until morning. . . ."

Alys switched it off. They had all had enough of this kind of talk to last them a lifetime.

Claudia shivered. "If Thia Pendriel is making those earthquakes I wish Morgana would stop her."

Alys gasped. "Janie!"

"Yes! *Where's the epicenter?*"

Alys stabbed wildly at the radio controls.

". . . centered in Point Reyes but felt as far away as San Jose. We'll have an update at midnight—"

"Find it!" shouted Alys, throwing the map over her shoulder in Janie's general direction as she sped out the next exit, heading north again.

Janie shook the map open, simultaneously clouting the bewildered Claudia on the shoulder. "Aristotle! Albert Einstein! What a genius!" she said.

Claudia looked as if she might try to jump out of the car while it was still moving. "What's going on?" she wailed. "I don't understand! Where are we going?"

"To the place where Thia Pendriel's got to be if she's causing the quakes. To the place where Morgana's got to be if she followed her. To Point Reyes, you silly child. Point Reyes!"

▾   ▾   ▾

When the initial exhilaration had worn off, Alys once again found her jaw aching and her eyes blurring.

"Let me drive a while."

"I'm fine, Janie." The car wove and hit speed bumps on the left-hand side. She overcorrected and suddenly they were bumping along the gravel shoulder. She hit the brakes and they stopped.

"Yes, I can see you are. Now get out and let me do it. I'm perfectly competent, you know."

Janie didn't even have a temporary permit, Alys reflected as she stretched out in the backseat. Ah, well, she thought, if anyone tries to give her a ticket she can just turn them into a ring-tailed lemur. Morrow Krinkle Frazetta.

▾   ▾   ▾

In the dark and majestic wood Morgana lightly touched each of the ward anchors in turn, gazing earnestly up into the night sky. She could not hear the *Fava-se-rá*, but something set her skin to prickling. She had not slept last night, but she was completely awake and alert.

Her vigil was almost over. Thia Pendriel, her old rival, the Guildmistress who could not be content with the most powerful Silver Staff in the Wildworld, had failed. By this time tomorrow she would be in irons or in exile—and Morgana would be responsible. Even armed with a Gem, the councillor could not defeat her.

Because the wards were impregnable. Enclosure, entrapment, the control or diversion of power—these had always been Morgana's forte. And the ground on which she stood thrummed with the power she had set in it. *A savage place, as holy and enchanted / as e'er beneath a waning moon was haunted / by woman wailing for her demon lover,* she thought.

Nothing from outside could get in.

She was thinking this as the clocks in San Francisco struck twelve. At that moment her skin prickled again. She sprang up, her instincts warning her clearly at last, but it was too late. The explosion of power slammed into her from behind. The wards collapsed on her at once, cradling her in invisible armor, knocking her unconscious before she could even cry out. She was unharmed, but her mind fell into darkness.

▼ ▼ ▼

The latter years of Arthur's reign were painful. Merlin, for all his power and elaborate scheming, was gradually supplanted in Arthur's affections by the most unlikely person imaginable—Guinevere. Guinevere was shy, plain, and modest, and had been chosen as queen by Merlin for exactly those qualities. She was also gentle, loyal, and unfailingly honest, qualities which escaped Merlin entirely but which captured Arthur's heart, especially as Merlin was now so often whimsical and unreliable.

Morgana believed that had the sorcerer undertaken to restore Arthur's full faith in him he would easily have succeeded. Arthur was like that. Instead, as time went on Merlin's behavior only became more and more erratic. If he could not have Arthur's sole confidence as a friend, at least he would have Arthur's attention as a troublemaker. This worked well enough at first, but gradually he had to go to greater and greater extremes to achieve the same effect. What had started as a means to an end eventually became an end in itself. He was no longer working mischief in order to make Arthur make him stop. He was doing it because he enjoyed it.

Apprehensive, Morgana sent one of her apprentices to spy on him. Viviane was her best, with a mind like bright steel and hair like copper. But though Merlin might by then have lost his sanity he had not lost his charm. The girl fell in love with him, and her reports to Morgana were virtually useless.

Worst of all, Morgana suspected—no, she *knew*—that Merlin was surreptitiously using the Gem. The effects on him, the paranoia and madness, were unmistakable. The effects were apparent in Arthur's court as well—or perhaps what happened was merely the result of human nature. It scarcely mattered; the end was going to be the same. Arthur's dream was falling apart at his feet.

Slowly at first, old feuds over land and honor resurfaced. Old grudges flared up and new ones developed. The rumors Merlin had started long ago about Lancelot's love for Guinevere by now had worked their way like a poison through the court. The Knights of the Table were divided and fought one against the other. Only Arthur, trying as always to love and trust everyone, refused to see what lay ahead.

It was Morgana who opened his eyes at last. She had no choice. Sketchy though Viviane's reports had become, it was clear that Merlin had tired of petty intrigues and minor harassments. He had already succeeded in driving Lancelot from Arthur's side; now he succeeded in making Lancelot

Arthur's enemy. He even lent secret aid to the army Lancelot was raising.

Telling Arthur was one of the hardest things she had done in her life. He was alone by then, Guinevere having been sent back to Wales for her own safety; Lancelot waiting on his borders to attack.

"I am sorry," Morgana said when she had finished. In her house his blue eyes had shone with self-assurance, conviction, and determination. Now the assurance was gone, but to Morgana's shock the conviction and determination were not. Arthur was not giving up. It was then that she knew what had to be done with Merlin.

To Chaos with the Council and the Council's rules. Their methods were too slow and she feared it might already be too late. She summoned Viviane and cast a portal.

The place she chose for Merlin was twilit even at midday. Far from the cultivated fields of England, far from the joyous festivity of May Day, Viviane had lured him. Morgana sat and absorbed the stillness and the beauty around her as she waited for the girl to return.

"It's done," said Viviane quietly, appearing from the shadows of the great trees like a wood sprite of the Wildworld. Her head was high, her sea green eyes remote. Morgana would have said, "I'm sorry," to her, too, but she walked on past without another word, without a glance. Her copper hair flared in a column of sunshine just before she was lost to sight.

Morgana went to him.

On the ground before the tree lay Viviane's White Staff, broken in two pieces. Broken, Morgana knew, by her own hand. Beside it among the sheltering leaves were Merlin's Gold and the sword he had stolen from Arthur.

From the depths of the hollow where he stood, frozen into near-stillness already, Merlin smiled at her.

"What a wonderful trick," he said. "How I wish I had thought of it first."

Morgana picked up his Gold Staff and slipped it in beside him. The thick reddish brown bark had already reached his waist and was quietly creeping upward. A tendril of thorny blackberry vine wound about the staff, binding it to him.

"And using Viviane, too. That was very clever. And so amusing for you both, I'm sure."

Morgana said steadily, "Viviane is gone. Although the Passage to Weerien is only a few miles away I don't think that's where she is going. I do not expect to see her again."

Merlin dropped his eyes. His breathing, normally so quick and light, was slowing.

Morgana picked up the sword. Mirror of Heaven flashed and shimmered in the perpetual twilight.

"All this," chided Merlin gently, "when you might simply have asked for it nicely."

Morgana glanced up. He was looking at her again. "I did," she said. "Don't you remember?"

"Ah, yes, so you did."

Morgana drove the blade into the ground and watched the bark begin to encase it. Such heavy bark, nearly a foot thick. It would be safe, as would he.

"I never wanted the Gem, Merlin, not for myself. And I would rather hold harmless than destroy. You know that."

"Morgana the Merciful. But has it occurred to you that

I would rather be destroyed than held harmless?"

Fuzzy-leafed thimbleberry crept up to his chest. At his feet clumps of wild iris and sorrel were rising. Morgana watched them and didn't answer.

When she looked up she was shocked to see he was laughing. Those long-lashed eyes were heavy.

"At home," he explained, still chuckling, "they are decorating the trees. Here, the trees are decorating *me*. I am a Maypole."

Morgana's throat closed. She steadied herself against the trunk. "Merlin. Oh, Merlin. If I let you out . . ."

"I would go on exactly as I have always done. But you know that, don't you, Morgana? You can't ever let me out, can you?" The furrowed red bark had nearly reached his shoulders by now. He leaned his head back to breathe slowly and deeply, eyelids drooping shut.

"No, Merlin. I can't."

"But . . . will you just stay with me a while?" All at once he sounded very young, almost afraid.

"As long as you like." Honeysuckle vines just barely brushed his chin.

"I have really been tired for quite some time now. I think perhaps it is best to have a rest."

"Yes, Merlin." His face was pale and beautiful against the red-brown background, his lashes dark crescents on his cheeks. Below, both the sword and the staff had been swallowed by the wood.

He gave one last flashing smile. "A rest—yes, perhaps that is best now."

They stood for a while in silence. Red trumpets of flowering currant caressed his silver hair.

Suddenly his eyes were open. "Morgana."

His voice was very soft, those mocking eyes no longer mocking. For a moment she saw once again the earnest young man she had seen in Ygraine's birthing chamber, the one who had said, "Hurt him? This is Arthur of Britain."

"You will . . . save him, won't you? Arthur?"

"Merlin, I—"

"Promise me." His breathing was almost stilled now, his hair garlanded with woodroses and tiny clusters of elderberry blossoms. "You must help him. The army . . ."

"I know, Merlin. Lancelot—"

"Not Lancelot. The other."

Morgana felt a chill inside. "What other? Merlin, what have you done?"

"The other . . . that is to attack at dusk . . ."

Here, it was midmorning. But in England, half a world away, twilight was falling.

Anger shook her. "How could you, Merlin? How could you have done this? And *why*?"

He seemed not to hear her. He seemed, in memory, to be reliving times long past. "Such a great king . . . so important . . . to train the child . . . keep the child . . ."

She leaned closer to catch the whisper, but it trailed off into silence. The living wall rose between them, and over it all the flowers of spring. She was alone.

And, though she cast portal after portal in a mad expenditure of power, she was too late. By the time she reached England, Arthur was dying.

The knights tending him on the field of battle gave way before her, watching her with frightened eyes. She knelt beside him.

"Is it . . . done?" He spoke with great effort.

The tears Morgana had held back with Merlin could be held back no longer. "Yes, Your Majesty. It is done."

"He . . . didn't suffer?"

"No," she whispered, and watched him nod once, content. She followed his feeble gesture toward a gleam of silver on the ground.

"Lady . . . your gift. I have no need of swords now. . . ."

When she took it he sank back and closed his eyes. Then, very softly: "Guinevere . . ."

He could say no more, but he didn't need to. She understood.

"Your Majesty, I will protect her. I will keep her safe as long as she lives."

Arthur smiled.

Later, it would be said that the Lady of the Lake and two other beautiful maidens dressed in black came in a barge to carry the body of King Arthur over the sea to Avalon. This was not true. Morgana had made a promise to protect the living. It was a promise she kept as best she could.

▼ ▼ ▼

In the red convertible speeding north Alys stirred and moaned, her head tossing. Janie, behind the wheel, heard it but did not look back. Her eyes stayed fixed grimly on the roadway, except when dropping even more grimly to glance again at her wrist.

Alys had been having nightmares for some time, but no amount of shaking or shouting would wake her. And on Janie's wrist, the crystal in her bracelet had shattered.

FIFTEEN

The Old Straight Track

"Claudia." Janie spoke without taking her eyes off the road. "I think I remember from last summer that we have to drive through San Francisco to get to Point Reyes. Look in the glove compartment and see if there's a map of the city."

Claudia rubbed her fist over her eyes. "Ummmm . . ." she said, trying to sound too sleepy to do it.

"It's easy. Just pull out all the maps and see if one says *San Francisco* in big white letters on the front. First just look for S A N, okay?" Janie's voice was impatient, and Claudia flinched, fingertips tracing the outline of the amulet under her shirt. But it could not help her now.

Slowly, she pulled out the maps and looked at them in despair. Big white letters swam and muddled in her mind.

Even more impatiently: "All right, *you* spell it for *me*. Read out the white letters you see." When Claudia made no answer she snapped, "What's the matter with you? Can't you read?"

Claudia swallowed and thought of black letters on white pages, swimming and muddling in Mrs. Anderson's classroom. Getting backward and out of order. She bowed her head.

Janie glanced at her sharply. Eyes back on the road, she said, "But you read at school. You have a reader."

"I guess a lot," said Claudia in a small voice. "And—I copy the other kids. . . ." It was only when she had to read by herself that she had trouble. It was like a secret code everyone understood but her. She swallowed again.

"Why didn't you *tell* anybody?"

Claudia shook her head. Until this year she had thought letters were like that for everyone, jumping around and mixing themselves up every time your back was turned. "I didn't want anybody to think I was stupid." She looked at Janie pleadingly. Didn't want anybody to *know* I was stupid, she added in her own mind.

"You're not stupid," said Janie. She said it without emotion, but it woke a spark of warmth in Claudia.

"You really think I'm not?"

"I know you're not. You may have a learning disability. That's something that can make it harder for you to learn to read. But it doesn't make you stupid. There are special books, special classes that can help if you do have one. When we get home we'll talk with Mom and Dad about it. And with your teacher."

The tiny warmth grew and spread, filling Claudia's chest. Maybe she *could* learn to read after all. She'd never be smart like Janie, but . . . just to read, like the other kids, to break that secret code! Right now she wouldn't even mind talking with Mrs. Anderson. Right now if she saw her she would probably hug her.

"That's when we get home." Janie's voice brought her

back to reality. "Right now we'd better pull over. I need a map and it's time I checked in the visioning circle again. Get that rabbit ready."

"His name," said Claudia, surprising herself, "is Benjamin."

Ten minutes later, Janie looked up from the shaving mirror, violet eyes dark and worried.

"What is it?"

"Two very, very big hot spots of power. One near Point Reyes, yes. But another one much nearer. Just north of San Francisco, over the Golden Gate Bridge." Janie's voice hardened. "And I've never seen anything like it in my life."

▾ ▾ ▾

". . . lys? Thank heavens. No, don't go ba . . ."

". . . 'mon now. Just please try . . ."

"*Alys!*"

Alys sat bolt upright, heart pounding. The dark outside the car was full of tall, shadowy shapes. Tall? Towering. There were trees at Point Reyes, but . . .

"Where are we?"

"So," said Janie dryly. "You've finally decided to join the living. We're at Muir Woods."

"What? *Why?*"

"Because," said Janie, "something very big has happened here. And because Morgana is in trouble." She held the heavy bracelet aloft. Alys blinked at it stupidly, still feeling half-asleep. "To give you an idea of how big," continued Janie, "look at this." The shaving mirror was one solid blaze of green with only threads of reddish background.

"Makes Elwyn and the entire Wild Hunt look like fireflies in comparison," she said.

Alys nodded, but she scarcely heard the last words. Her attention was turned inward. She didn't know how, but she *knew* Morgana was in trouble. She sensed it. She raised her eyes to meet Janie's.

"Looks like that thing won't be much help in getting an exact location for us."

"You're right. This whole place is supersaturated with magic. But there *is* a center to it somewhere. We'll just have to do our best and hope."

Alys reached down for the sword, then gasped and dropped it. It hadn't done *that* since the first time she'd touched it. She rubbed her arm, then, jaw set, reached again. This time she was able to keep her hold on it.

"Let's go."

They took a few things from the car with them. The flashlight. Janie's virtue wand. A few granola bars. Benjamin, who didn't want to go but yielded, trembling, to Claudia's persuasion.

Alys had hiked through Muir Woods before. In the daylight. On the trails. This was different.

They steered clear of the campsites, heading away from the one fire pit they glimpsed in the distance. At first they followed a trail, but presently, after a doubtful consultation with the rabbit, Janie led them off it into the damp pungent world beneath the trees. She was the only one who could see much, having the flashlight. Alys felt a twinge at leaving the trail behind. It was their last connection to civilization, to normal life, to outside help. Once in the wood they were on their own.

The great trees stood all around them like sentinels. Furrowed trunks soared straight up for thirty or forty feet before branching to form a canopy that obscured the sky. Fortunately, few plants could live in the perpetual dimness below, and so the underbrush was not as thick as it might have been. Still, Alys found herself dragging the heavy sword through low-growing ferns and over and under trunks that had fallen or, for some reason, chosen to grow horizontally. She gritted her teeth against the ache in her arm.

The only sounds to be heard were the steady crunch and crackle of their footsteps and the occasional grunt of effort. And—a creaking. Alys, without knowing it, slowed her pace to listen. It was not like the creaking of a door hinge or gate. It was much louder, deeper, almost a moan.

"It's the *trees,*" said Claudia, a note of hysteria in her voice. Alys realized the others had stopped, too.

"Never mind," she said, trying to sound reassuring and pushing away the picture of one of those giant columns creaking and tearing and crashing down. "It probably always sounds like this."

"No, it doesn't." Claudia was almost sobbing. "It's too *quiet.* There aren't any *animals.*"

Alys realized this was true. Standing silent like this she heard nothing but the groan of the trees, and, very, very far away, the screech of a horned owl.

"They've been frightened off—" began Janie, but she stopped and they all gasped. So quickly that it was over before they could react, the world had lit up. Every leaf, every needle, was illuminated from above and behind. And for that instant the black forest had turned green, not just ordinary green, but a neon, ultra, *incandescent* spring green medley. Benjamin thrashed in Claudia's arms, trying to thump his back feet. While they were still gaping a crash of thunder split the sky.

"Must be right above us," said Janie.

It didn't matter much. The woods were already damp and the canopy protected them. But every so often that flash would come, searing their eyes for an instant, banishing the shadows, showing them just how far away the treetops really were. And the thunder was deafening.

Every so often Janie would stop to consult with Benjamin and Claudia. At last, under a massive tree decked with lichen, they stopped dead.

"He's tired," said Claudia, near tears herself. "And he never wanted to come in the first place and he only did it because he loves me and he's *terrified.*"

"I don't *care* if he's terrified. I want a straight answer! Which way?"

Claudia knelt in the grass and bent close over Benjamin. He was trembling with exhaustion and it occurred to Alys suddenly that he was probably no longer saying anything at all. When Claudia at last looked up, Alys felt sure.

"That way," Claudia said, pointing defiantly.

Alys followed the gesture, then she shook her head. "No. This way."

"Alys—"

"It's not just bossiness, Janie. I *know*. Don't ask me how, but I do." She tried to peer through the shadows at Janie's skeptical face. "Will you once," she added wryly, "just please trust me?"

There was a silence. Then, with a sigh, Janie surrendered. She handed Alys the flashlight.

Purposefully, not daring to explore the sensation of *knowing* too closely lest she lose it, Alys led them on. At times the scent of crushed bay leaves rose around them as they passed through a space left open by the redwoods. Twice they had to cross small creeks, scooting precariously along the moss-covered trunks that spanned the icy water only to struggle through wet masses of bracken on the other side. Claudia fell in.

They came to a clearing ringed with laurel trees.

"Very close," said Alys, and then: "Morgana!"

They ran to her, the flashlight wavering crazily. She was lying on her side, turned away from them, the Gold Staff hugged close to her body. Her eyes were shut, her skin pale against the blanket of dark green needles. Alys bent over her and then a flash of lightning illuminated the scene behind her.

"What *happened*?" gasped Claudia.

Alys could only shake her head dumbly, the details of that image seared on her eyelids. A tree, a monolithic tree, towering, majestic, its living heart exploded outward. What was left was a gaping charred hollow in the trunk with smoldering strips of bark still clinging to the edges of the hole. The entire clearing was littered with splinters blown outward by the blast.

"He got out," she said, answering the question at last.

"*Who?*"

Alys turned the flashlight on Janie and saw that Janie knew. "Someone unfriendly," she said, reaching for Morgana.

She meant to shake her. She couldn't. She couldn't even touch the little sorceress. A thin, almost greasy-feeling shield resisted her fingers. It was as if a layer of air only molecules thick separated them from Morgana's skin.

"The wards have collapsed," said Janie, squatting beside Alys. Her face was bleak.

Alys read that expression without difficulty. "And you can't uncollapse them."

"Not without a Silver Staff at the very least. A Gem of Power would be more like it."

"You opened a rent in our wards at home."

"I loosened one of the ward anchors for a few minutes. Alys, those wards were strong enough for our purposes, but they were only a double-layered octagon. Only seventeen anchor points, including the central one. This shield of Morgana's has *one hundred eighty-two*, and every one of them as tough as steel. Nothing can get through that, not sound or light or touch or magic."

What about memory, thought Alys. The fragments of dreams, scenes like snapshots which flickered as suddenly as the lightning behind her closed lids, were clearer now. They came more frequently. Scarcely aware of what she was doing, she leaned over and placed both hands on Morgana's back. She shut her eyes.

"Alys . . . ?"

She ignored it. Sun on the lake near the Forest of Darnantes. The darkness of Tintagel tower at night. Silver eyes and a heartbreakingly terrible smile. A Gem that glowed blue like the sky at midmorning.

"Go on," whispered Janie behind her. "You're doing it."

The swirl of a gray cloak, the sound of mocking laughter. The coppery smell of blood on a battlefield, the salty taste of tears. Blue eyes, weary and sad, gazing beyond her. And the Gem, the Gem that brought destruction, the stone in the sword . . .

Something melted away beneath her fingers and she was touching warm cloth. With a twitch and a sneeze Morgana rolled over, opening wide dark eyes.

She and Alys stared at each other. Then a flash of lightning blinded and when Alys could see again the little sorceress was on her feet, gazing into the sky above the clearing intently, body taut as a bow.

"I should have realized you'd come," she said at last, her attention abruptly back on them. Her eyes dropped to the sword, and she nodded, unsurprised. She swept Janie and Claudia with a glance.

"We got chased out," said Janie. "Thia Pendriel sent boojums."

"And so of course you at once made for a place of safety," said Morgana dryly. Then she shook her head. "Never mind. Of course, I am grateful, and once again in your debt. But I must go now, and you cannot follow me. Merlin will have joined Thia Pendriel by now. If they force the Passage open and get through to Weerien the Council will not know to stop them. And they must be stopped."

"But can't we—"

"No! You children *stay*. Stay *here*. With the vixen." She

glanced around, a line appearing between her brows. "Where is the vixen?"

Janie froze. "She . . . well, she—"

"There's no time now. We'll discuss it later. Try to get out of the woods if you can. Things are about to happen. Now stand back!"

Alys had seen a portal cast before. It was not, however, the sort of thing you got used to. Morgana thrust out the Gold Staff and a light sizzled from it, corkscrewing to outline a helix that swirled and dazzled like a tunnel of gold. It punched straight through the trees and extended as far as the eye could see north. While they were all still gasping Morgana stepped into the tunnel and it disappeared.

"You're welcome," shouted Alys as the last bit of gold winked out. They were left alone with the flashlight and the cherry red embers surrounding the charred hollow. Janie stood, gazing, as Morgana had, at the northern sky.

"Now what's *that?*" snarled Alys, offended, when she followed her gaze.

Janie, eyes on the ribbons of rainbow-hued light which could barely be seen above the trees at the edge of the clearing, shrugged. "The aurora borealis?" she offered.

"We're not *that* far north."

The ground lurched below them.

"I think Morgana has arrived."

"But how do *we* get there?"

Janie, suddenly serene, turned to face her. "You know, you *are* crazy," she said equably. "I don't know. Let's sit down and think."

▾   ▾   ▾

Elwyn was gazing down at the Pacific Ocean, white-tipped waves crashing far below. "There. I told you you'd like it."

Charles eased himself gingerly to the edge of the precipice. Lightning flickered somewhere near the horizon. "Oh, sure I like it. But I've got to go back now. And how do we get *down*?" He turned back to Elwyn who was watching him, cerulean eyes fixed on his face, moonlit hair blowing about her. It made him feel strange.

"Do you like *me*?" said Elwyn abruptly. He hadn't expected her to answer his question; Elwyn never answered questions. He didn't see why it should bother him now. "Because," she said, softly, "I like you."

She was deranged, birdwitted, weak in the upper story. She was also ravishingly pretty and smelled like night-blooming jasmine. Before Charles had the first idea what he was going to do, he had grabbed her and kissed her.

Elwyn laughed blithely. An indescribable sound, thought Charles dizzily, something between birds and bells. She leaned over and kissed him back.

"Listen," said Charles, sitting down hard. "I've got to get back to my sisters."

"Shoosh," said Elwyn, sinking gracefully down herself. She sparkled, glowed, lilted when she talked. He leaned forward and shut his eyes.

Lightning flashed red against his closed lids, and thunder cracked like a mirror being broken. Charles jerked back. "There aren't any *clouds.*"

Elwyn looked up, then down. "It's that Gem thing," she said patiently. "It does thus when wielded."

"What? Heart of Valor?" He leaped up.

Elwyn now looked disconsolate—and, yes, vexed. "No," she said, frowning, "the other."

"What? Never mind. Elwyn, I've got to get over there. To wherever it is the Gem is being used. No—wait; I've got to get to my sisters, first. *Elwyn,*"—he took her by the shoulders and shook her, looking into that forget-me-not gaze—"Elwyn, I know this is hard for you, but for the love of Mike will you please try to tune in for a second? I need you to listen to me."

▾   ▾   ▾

Alys, Janie, and Claudia were standing very wetly in the middle of a clearing when the elk appeared. Charles grinned at them in triumph and jumped down.

Explanations were exchanged hastily. While this was happening Alys was eyeing Elwyn, which caused Charles to experience a sinking feeling of responsibility. He had brought her, and now it was up to him to make her be useful.

"That elk," said Alys. "Are there any like it?"

"More elk?" Elwyn looked at Alys as if suspecting she had taken leave of her senses. Then her face cleared. "Oh! You're hungry. I could—"

"We are not *hungry,*" said Alys. Things were not looking so good; she'd been reduced to yelling by the second sentence. "We are in need of *transportation.*"

"To where?" said Elwyn, even more blankly than before.

"To the Passage that leads to Weerien! To the place where Morgana is probably fighting for her life with Thia Pendriel and Merlin this minute!"

Elwyn looked cautious, and Charles had a dreadful feeling that she was going to ask why. But "why?" was not a question that often occurred to Elwyn.

"What's wrong with the straightway?" was what she said, after a moment. She said it hesitantly, as if embarrassed about putting forward so obvious a solution.

"The what? What is it? *Where* is it?"

Elwyn looked at them doubtfully. She really was trying, Charles could tell. It occurred to him for the first time that these conversations were as difficult for Elwyn as for the rest of them.

"Where is it?" she repeated, with exactly the same intonation Alys might have used if Janie had demanded *Where's my head?* Then she suddenly looked both pleased and crafty. "It's a riddle?"

"Oh, God," said Alys.

"Look," said Charles to Elwyn hastily. "Is it around here? Can you just point to it?"

"Point to it." Elwyn gave a small, wan smile, and pointed upward, her eyes still on them. Her expression now said that they were obviously dangerous lunatics who must be humored. *(Where's my head, dang it? It must be around here somewhere!)* She said helplessly, "It's those lines. You see the lines?"

"No!" said Charles. In his frustration he grabbed her by one fragile shoulder. "I don't—"

He did.

He let go of her, stared, and clutched her again. He stood still, gaping upward. "Alys. Touch her. Then look."

Alys gingerly laid a hand on Elwyn's other shoulder. She

gasped. Claudia grabbed Alys's hand and gasped too.

Janie walked quietly up to Charles and linked an arm through his, completing the chain. She looked up.

It was a latticework of lines thin as spider webs, gleaming like gold or silver though they were neither of these colors. A delicate lace skein stretching from horizon to horizon and as far up as they could see. It was the cosmic cat's cradle, the warp and woof of time and space.

Alys tore her gaze down from it to look at Elwyn. "Are you saying that can take us to Weerien?"

"Oh, no," Elwyn said promptly.

Before Alys could take a swing at her Charles broke in. "Can it take us anywhere? Like to the Passage?"

"Oh, yes," said Elwyn, just as promptly.

"Okay, let's go! Let's go now!" he said gaily, taking a small shuffling step with his arm still linked through Elwyn's. As he had hoped, Elwyn smiled blithesomely and stepped out with him, and the next moment she was actually leading the rest of them. She stepped onto one of the spider webs and Charles suddenly saw it change, not as if it were growing, but as if it were rotating in space, as if what he had seen at first was an edge-on plane. It was now a glimmering road like a moonpath on still water, and as he stepped on it he instantly had the sense of moving swiftly but very smoothly. Wind blew in his face, bringing a tang of salt to his lips.

"The old straight track," murmured Janie. He looked at her and smiled.

▾ ▾ ▾

SIXTEEN

The Archon

The straight path was curving downward toward earth.

"Where are we?" shouted Alys. They took the last step at a jump and landed (except Elwyn) hard on hands and knees. When they'd picked themselves up the straightway had disappeared.

"Somewhere at Point Reyes," said Janie, looking around.

They were on a little spit of sand, a mini-peninsula bounded on three sides by water. The sky above them was quite an ordinary sky, filled with distant, winking stars. No auroral streamers and ribbons, no lightning. And the silence was formidable.

Janie was peering toward the dark rise of the mainland. "This is probably the northernmost point of the Passage," she said. "And of the fault. This particular bit of land isn't really attached to *that* land at all. It's an island riding the Pacific plate, and in a few million years it should reach Alaska."

Alys was impatient with the lecture. "Where are *they?*"

"Gone through, I suspect. Elwyn. I need your help. Is the Passage that way? Is it open?"

Elwyn's jewel blue gaze fixed on something beyond Janie. "Just a crack," she said.

"Then that's it. That last quake must have done it. They've gone through. Do we follow?"

Alys nodded, peering into the direction Elwyn was looking, surprised. She'd expected the searing blue light of the mirrors or the golden turbulence of a portal. But the Passage showed as the merest distortion in the darkness, a rippling as if she were looking at objects beyond through a shimmer of hot air.

"It's not like the mirrors," Janie explained. "It can't be approached directly. We have to be at precisely the right angle to get through the 'crack.'"

Elwyn, after some initial misunderstanding, was persuaded to help in this. But as they moved forward, hands linked again, she broke away.

"Aren't you coming?"

"There?" Elwyn stared at Charles in amazement. "Why that will take you into Weerien, to the path which leads to the Council itself!"

"Perfect," said Alys, relieved. The Weerul Council, though stern, was just. They had sent a phalanx of Feathered Serpents to Morgana's aid last year. Once they understood about Thia Pendriel they would be able to deal with her.

Elwyn was still shaking her head wonderingly. "They are *no fun*," she said, and watched in pity as Janie led the others into the heat-shimmer. That was the last thing Alys saw as she stepped from darkness into light: Elwyn's expression of sorrowful bewilderment.

It was the same spit of land, the same ordinary night sky

above. But the stars here were feeble candles dimmed by a wash of light from all directions. They stood between two pillars in a vast line of pillars which stretched west into the distance until they met a white building on a hill. A soft radiance shone from the pillars themselves, illuminating the marble pathway.

No sign of Morgana. No sign of anyone. They were alone in this deserted colonnade of light.

"Stand as you are."

Alys, with a prickling feeling raising the fine hairs on her neck, stood as she was, the others freezing beside her. Carefully, slowly, she turned her head to see the two armed and helmeted sorcerei behind them.

▾   ▾   ▾

It was a long walk to the seat of the Council, the white building she had seen in the distance. The guards would not talk to them. Shortly after capturing the children one of the two had lifted her arm, and what had looked like a long, spiraling black bracelet set with coral gems had unwound itself and wheeled off into the sky. Alys's breath caught as she watched it. *Her* serpent had been just about that size, had coiled around her arm in just that way. She wondered what had become of it. With Morgana's house destroyed it would have had nothing left to guard. Perhaps, like this messenger, it had been employed by the Council.

The white building turned out to be a walled citadel. As they got closer the colonnade curved up a slight gradient until they reached an enormous gate inlaid with what might have been ebony and ivory. It swung open soundlessly for the guards and on the other side they could see terraced gardens, one above the other, with flights of broad steps ascending toward a central dome. There were no people, nothing moved except themselves. It was like a scene from a dream.

At the top of the steps was another door, decorated like the first. Above it was a marble slab bearing an inscription Alys could not read. They went through it to find themselves in a long passage paved with marble.

White. Everything was white. And silent. It was, Alys thought, gripping Claudia's hand more tightly, like a giant carved-ice sculpture. Even the woman who approached them from the opposite end of the corridor was dressed in white, and there was a White Staff in her hand.

Alys was glad to see someone other than the taciturn guards, and this woman's face was kind. But as she reached them Alys's attention focused on the staff she held. In her mind she saw a white staff, lying in two pieces on the forest floor. . . .

She snapped her gaze up to the woman's face. Smooth brown hair instead of copper. Steady hazel eyes instead of sea green. Not Viviane, then . . .

"I am Terzian Logren."

Startled, Alys glanced at Janie. Terzian Logren was the cousin of Cadal Forge, the one who had begged Morgana to help him long ago. Morgana's friend. An ally. It was all Alys could do to keep from leaping forward and hugging her.

"We've come after Morgana. Have you seen her? And Thia Pendriel. Did they catch her?" She realized she was babbling. She took a deep breath and pulled herself together. "We are humans, from the Stillworld," she said very carefully. "My name is Alys—"

"I know you full well. The Council has had report of your doings last winter. You are Alys; you, Charles; you, Janie; and you, Claudia."

Alys was even more startled. After the solstice she'd had daydreams about being famous in Weerien, with epic poems and ballads written about her. The daydreams had been pleasant. The reality, however, was disconcerting.

"You know all about us?"

"Not all. Enough. And, as for your other questions, yes, I have seen both Morgana and Magistress Thia. They are even now with the Council. I have been dispatched to bring you to them."

The adrenaline rush that had kept Alys alert and focused since finding Morgana faded in a wave of relief. All at once she could feel her weariness, and she was glad this would soon be over. Thia Pendriel and Merlin were now the Council's problem.

"Lead on," she said, with a tired but triumphant smile. As they continued down the corridor she noted through the pleasant fuzziness that had descended on her that Janie looked tense and not at all triumphant. Trust Janie to throw a damper on a celebratory occasion. . . . No.

She pulled up short. "What is it, Janie? What's wrong?"

"I hope I am." Janie's violet eyes were fixed on the third pair of great doors, which was now before them. "We'll find out soon enough. There's nothing to do about it anyway. We've got to go through with it."

"Janie . . ." And that was all she said. The doors opened silently and they went through.

▼ ▼ ▼

Another room of ice white, smelling like clean snow. Alys's stomach had begun to sink at Janie's words; as she stepped into the room it was as if a cold wind slapped her in the face, leaving her nervy and wide-awake.

The floor was so decorated with polished marble and pearls that she could almost imagine it was made of running water. The domed ceiling was the same. Around the circular walls ran a gently ascending spiral of niches, and in every niche was a sinuous shape. Feathered Serpents of various sizes, Alys realized. The Guardians of the Council. Against the alabaster of the walls they stood out in startling detail, down to the last scale and clawed wingtip.

As they drew nearer to the far side of the room Alys could see twelve chairs, or thrones, on a dais. The sorcerei ensconced there stood out against the white background, too, in colored robes which had the transparent shimmer of milky glass. Other sorcerei, most of them younger, were stationed here and there between the chairs, and there were even a few animals: a panther with a gold collar, a peacock, several hawklike birds. Four of the chairs were empty, three on one side and one just to the right of the central seat. Three for the three ancient councillors who went mad, thought Alys, and one for . . .

Thia Pendriel. She stood quietly before the dais, as stately and beautiful as Alys remembered her. Her hair, so dark a red that it was almost purple, was coiled in braids on her head, her silver circlet still glittered. And she still wore her favorite colors, midnight blue shot with silver. A slender chain, thin as a necklace, bound her hands together in front of her. It looked symbolic, but Alys would have bet money it wasn't. Most likely it was magical, for without her staff or other implements a sorceress was as helpless as anyone against magic. And Thia Pendriel's Silver Staff lay on the ground before the central seat.

But so did a Gold. Not Merlin's. A Gold which, away from the hand of its mistress, lost its life and shimmer and looked like nothing so much as an old brass fireplace poker.

"Morgana!" said Claudia, and Alys clamped a hand on her arm to shut her up. Morgana was standing just opposite Thia Pendriel, looking rather small and unimportant among these stern and majestic figures, her hands also bound in front of her with that light chain. At Claudia's cry she glanced over her shoulder at them, and stiffened. The attention of the whole room was on them now.

Alys could feel her heart pounding in her throat. It was horrible to have all those dark, keen eyes on her, horrible to have to keep walking toward them in the dead silence. She wished, desperately, for something to hide behind.

Instead, she pushed Claudia behind her. The four of them, followed by Terzian, kept close together until they stood in the space between Morgana and Thia Pendriel, directly before the central seat.

The man enthroned there was white-haired, with compassionate, far-seeing eyes. And he was *old*. Though his face was not lined, his skin was thin and translucent as mica, so that the blue veins showed through. He wore a heavy band across his forehead, not a crown but a circle of metal encrusted with jewels.

"Archon, these are the ones who came through the Passage." Terzian's voice came from behind Alys, and the regret in it, and in the old man's face, caused another chill to sweep over Alys.

"Let them come forward one by one and lay down their weapons." *His* voice was surprisingly deep, measured and resonant.

I can't, thought Alys, I can't. She looked helplessly at Janie and saw that Janie understood and was bracing herself to step forward first.

"No," whispered Alys. She managed two stiff paces toward the Archon and bent to place Caliborn on the ground. "I—" she began, croaking.

"Alys Lawschildes of Irenahl, did you enter this world of your own will?"

How do they know my middle name, she thought, irrelevantly and with indignation. Irenahl meant the Stillworld. "Yes," she said, finally, feeling at a loss. Then, uncertainly, she stepped back. She was beginning to get an idea of what kind of trouble they were in.

One by one, the others went forward.

"Jane Eleanore of Irenahl, did you enter this world of your own will?"

"Yes." There was a murmur of recognition and disapproval at the sight of Janie's virtue wand.

"Charles Edward of Irenahl, did you enter this world of your own will?"

"Yes." Charles lifted empty—and somewhat grimy—hands to show the room he was unarmed, then raked those hands through his hair and shrugged. He walked back to his sisters, looking tense and grim.

"Claudia Diana of Irenahl, did you enter this world of your own will?"

Claudia moved forward perhaps an inch and nodded, mouth drawn into a button, chin wobbling. Then, following the gaze of the Archon, she clutched Benjamin even more tightly.

"Claudia, you have to," breathed Janie, exerting gentle pressure on her back. "Claudia, it's a familiar, and under their law it's technically a weapon."

"No," said Claudia flatly, blue eyes swimming. She looked up at the Archon and said it again. There was a heavy silence. Alys, casting a pleading glance at Morgana, was startled to see the little sorceress biting her lip. She might have been envisioning the tall Archon or one of his guards trying to wrestle the bunny from an eight-year-old's arms. Apparently several of the other councillors had the same picture, for there were repressed smiles here and there. The old man nodded slightly and Benjamin stayed where he was.

But those were the last smiles. Alys and her group were allowed to move back and watch some procedure that had clearly been underway when they entered. Alys could understand very little of it. Janie, her purple eyes flashing back and forth between speakers, seemed to be getting more.

"What is it? What's happening?"

"You haven't guessed yet? It's a trial."

Alys blinked and shook her head. "But where's Merlin?"

188

"Merlin?" said Terzian Logren from behind them. "Where should he be? And he dead these many hundreds of years."

"He isn't dead; Morgana trapped him. And Thia Pendriel let him out. Isn't that what she's on trial for?"

It was Terzian's turn to stare. "This is a trial of Morgana Shee, for crimes committed against the Council both last winter and tonight. Magistress Thia is a chief witness against her, but she also stands accused of derelicting her duties and causing a disturbance in Weerien by battling with Morgana in the streets tonight."

"Causing a disturbance? *Causing a disturbance?*" Alys's stomach lurched in disbelief. She was truly afraid, now. How could everything have gone so wrong?

"Know this." The Archon's voice rang out in tones which stopped the whispered conference at once. "The Council will now pronounce judgment. Four children of Irenahl have entered Findahl of their own will and in defiance of the laws of the Council. The penalty for this was set long ago. However, one of the children is a Stillworlder by birth only. He has been claimed by the Quislai and may abide by that kinship. Charles Edward, step forward."

Charles, slowly, did.

"Charles Edward, the Quislai and their chosen are not subject to the Council's law. If you wish, you may leave this place."

Charles's hand, as if involuntarily, went to his forehead where Elwyn's mark shone faintly. He turned to Alys and Janie and Claudia, looking uncomfortable.

"What's he mean?"

"He means you can get off," Janie hissed. "You can walk out of here right now."

"And what about you guys?"

"Don't ask stupid questions."

Charles stared a moment, and then a rather odd smile tugged at his lips. He faced the Archon again.

"No thanks," he said, tonelessly. "If it's all the same to you, I guess I'll just stay with my sisters." He stepped back, his blue eyes cool and proud. Alys took his hand and he let her.

What was it in the Archon's face? Regret, again? Reluctant admiration? It didn't matter; he was turning to Morgana now.

"Know this, that Morgana Shee, wielder of the Sun Gold, exile of Findahl, is found guilty of returning to this world against the Council's express decree, of teaching the Wild Arts to humans, and of inciting humans to defy the Council's law. These charges have been proved. Morgana, have you anything to say?"

"Yes." Morgana's voice was clear and unhurried. She had her back to Alys, her storm-cloud hair in disarray about her shoulders, her slight body drawn up into one pure line of scorn. "The proof of the charges lies all too clearly before you. I am here, therefore I am guilty. I have never asked for mercy from the Council—and never expected sense from it, either. But, I warn you, one of your magistrates is guilty of far greater crimes than I. And, I tell you, those four humans are infants whose wills are subject to my own. They are not responsible for their actions."

"Primitives seldom think for themselves. That has been

taken into consideration." But Alys saw the sadness in those old, dark eyes. Ice ran up and down her spine. Death, she thought. The penalty for humans who enter the Wildworld is death.

"Know this," the slow, resonant voice was continuing, "that Thia Pendriel, wielder of the Ice Silver, Magistrate of Findahl, is found guiltless of charges regarding her departure from this world and this night's disturbance. These acts were done in accordance with the Council's law and to restrain a known criminal." Alys stared in unbelief as an attendant stepped forward as if to undo the golden chains on Thia Pendriel's wrists. She turned to the others: Charles looked dazed, Claudia bewildered and frightened. Only Janie, teeth gnawing her lower lip, met her eyes.

"Why not?" she said to Alys, shrugging slightly. "We've got nothing to lose."

Breathing hard, Alys tried to clear her throat. Her voice still came out hoarse and rushed and tremulous.

"What about all the other things she's done?"

The attendant paused. Every eye in the room fixed on Alys.

The dark-haired young man with the panther lolling in front of him broke the silence. "There are no other charges against her."

"Well, maybe there should be. Or is it all right in this world to try to murder people, and to steal Gems of Power, and to plot with sorcerers like Cadal Forge—"

"Cease!" said the woman who sat on one side of the Archon, but Thia Pendriel spoke before she could go on.

"Magistress Zoe, I am as ignorant of these charges as you.

But I would hear them and answer them. I want there to be no doubt about the wisdom of the Archon's judgment." Her voice was as courteous as ever, and so reasonable that Alys almost found herself believing the words. "Now, child, speak."

Alys swallowed and began with difficulty. "You plotted with Cadal Forge to come into our world and take it over."

Light gleamed off the circlet as Thia Pendriel slowly shook her head. "No," she said gently. "I won Cadal Forge's trust so I could discover his plans. I tried to forestall him, and, failing that, followed him into your world to bring him to justice."

"You stole Heart of Valor!"

There were exclamations, not merely disapproving, now, but angry.

"Heart of Valor is one of the Forgotten Gems, destroyed long ago in the wars before the Time of Chaos."

"Cadal Forge had it, and you stole it—"

"Child," said Thia Pendriel gently, "If I had a Gem of Power, would I be here?" She lifted her bound hands in a small gesture of helplessness.

Yes, thought Alys, because you're getting away with all of it, aren't you? With everything you want.

"You sent creatures down after us. A shape shifter and hundreds of elementals. They nearly killed us."

"*I* did this?" the tall councillor said softly. "I? And how do you know that?"

Alys looked at Janie for support, but Janie was staring into space, eyes narrowed.

"You let Merlin out of the tree. And *he* has a Gem, too."

Furious, she bit her lip hard in anticipation of the councillor's answer. No proof. They knew perfectly well what Thia Pendriel had done, but there was no proof of any of it. As Janie had said so often, Thia Pendriel was smart.

"I have no idea of who or what you are talking about," said Thia Pendriel steadily, looking straight at her.

The woman beside the Archon, Magistress Zoe, leaned forward, face grave. "You speak again of the Gems of Power, young one. How can you know anything of them? They were all lost countless years ago, all but the three which are watched eternally by the Guardian here in the Serpent's Lair. They belong to no one, and no one, not even the Archon himself, could steal them from a Feathered Serpent."

"Those aren't the Gems I'm talking about! I'm talking about Heart of Valor and Mirror of Heaven—"

"Both lost."

"No they aren't!" But *we* are, thought Alys. Whatever it was Thia Pendriel wanted to do, she was succeeding with a vengeance. It was the word of four damp, grubby human criminals against hers.

The Archon put an end to it. "We have listened to your accusations. Have you any proof of what you say?"

Alys looked at the others miserably and hissed, "Where's Merlin? If we could find him, they'd believe us. And wherever he is, he's got Mirror of Heaven. And what about Heart of Valor? Where is *it*?"

There was no answer from any of them, though Janie's head came up abruptly.

Slowly, Alys turned back to the Archon. But before she

could speak, Janie did. Those purple eyes were no longer distant but blazing.

"Yes!" she said. "We do have proof! Or, at least, we can prove what we say." She reached a hand into her pocket and brought out a rather squashed plastic bag. Alys, wildly, wondered if she'd gone mad. "This is Worldleaf."

The Archon's face betrayed his surprise. "Worldleaf! How long has it been since that has grown in Findahl?"

"I don't know. Morgana has had hers stored for centuries. *We,*" said Janie carefully and precisely, "have only used it for persuading other people to believe us when we tell them the truth. But I don't see why it couldn't be used the other way around, to detect falsehood. Now, suppose"—she took a step toward Thia Pendriel—"I give this to the Archon, and you tell him your story again—"

Pandemonium broke out.

▼ ▼ ▼

SEVENTEEN

Mirror of Heaven

The thin gold chains around Thia Pendriel's wrists snapped like spider webs and a red light shone between her fingers. Alys knew what it was even before Janie spoke. Heart of Valor.

"*She* had it, of course."

The tall councillor, moving more swiftly than Alys would have thought possible, snatched up her Silver Staff. Just an instant behind her, Janie dove. Alys thought she was going for the virtue wand, but instead Morgana's staff was suddenly flying through the air. Morgana caught it and as the gold sparks swarmed through it her chains fell free. She turned it on Thia Pendriel, but two of the councillors, the dark man and Magistress Zoe, had their staffs aloft and raised against her. Allies of Thia Pendriel, Alys realized, profoundly shocked. The rest of the Council seemed also to have been shocked into stillness, but in an instant all that changed. Alys had a confused impression of swirling robes, diving serpents, shouting voices. Thia Pendriel was running, with Morgana after her. "Made" elementals, the creatures Janie had called boojums, were suddenly all around—silky eels and creeping slugs and trembling icicles of fire. Alys dove beside Janie and grabbed the sword and then tried to grab Janie, too.

"Come with me!"

"I have to go to Morgana!"

"Janie, no! Listen to me—" But Janie twisted away and was gone. Smoke or fog was rolling into the room in great swirling clouds, lit with the hyaline colors of sorcerous energy. Hands fell on Alys from behind and she screamed, and spun to see Charles. She seized him by the arm and then grabbed hold of Claudia. She could just barely make out a dark rectangle of doorway in one curving wall. They burst through into the night outside. Fog billowed after them.

"Sit down and stay here! Charles! Where's Morgana?"

"I don't know. I can't see anything!"

The fog had engulfed them, full of colored light. No, not fog, *mist*, thought Alys. She looked around wildly. "Janie! Janie, I need you!"

Something dropped on her out of the roiling vapors above. She threw up a hand to ward it off, and it coiled down her arm, wings collapsing to a flexible ridge along its back.

"My lady Alys . . ."

"It's *you!*"

Alys was dumbfounded. This was no illusion, this was her own serpent, looking just as it had when it had left her last year. Its blue and coral body poured itself back up her arm so that black-bead eyes could gaze lovingly into her face. "Oh, it really is you! You don't know how much I've missed you—" She broke off, tensing, her voice changing. "Or— how much I *need* you. Right now! Can you help me?"

The serpent hissed softly. "Lady, I owe you my life. Whatever you wish, I will do. You know that."

"Then take me to the Serpent's Lair. *Quickly.*" She

whirled back on Charles and Claudia. "You two stay here. If you see Janie and Morgana tell them where I am. I'm going to try to stop him."

"Stop *who?*" But she was already plunging back through the door, the serpent a flicker of blue and coral ahead.

She could barely follow it in the turbulent mist, but she sensed it was leading her through a pair of huge doors behind the dais. The mist thinned out in the downward-sloping passage beyond, until it was merely a swirling whiteness around her knees, obscuring the floor. She could feel that it was no longer slick marble but something like granite, which gave her traction. She ran until the corridor opened out into a chamber.

It was an enormous, lofty room, apparently carved out of the natural rock of the hill, and lit by torches in holders on the walls. The roof was supported by gigantic pillars of the same rock, which seemed to have been left in place when the chamber was excavated. The mist was not high enough to obscure the piles of gold and silver and raw stones on the floor. It looked exactly like the sort of grotto in which one would find a Feathered Serpent—or a host of them—but her own serpent was heading for a large archway at the back of the room. She struggled through the heaps of precious stuff which barked her shins like rocks.

Through the arch was another cavern, identical to the first except that the ground here was piled high with weapons. A third room held golden utensils for food and drink, and what looked like sorcerous implements. Winded and bruised, she paused an instant at the entrance to the fourth chamber.

This arch was higher than the others, and the light was blocked by a large wall a few steps inside. Alys put a hand to the wall, which curved up and away from her, and was surprised at its texture. It was warm and rough and gave slightly beneath her fingers. She looked right and left, uncertain.

"Is there a way to get past this? To get inside?"

The serpent alighted on her shoulder, tail coiled around her arm. "We are inside," it said. "But I can guide you to the center if you wish." At her nod it took off straight up, as if to get its bearings, then swooped down again to lead her down the left-hand path.

The curving wall on her right came very close to the granite wall on her left at times, and she had to turn sideways to slip through. She was in some kind of a labyrinth, she realized, whose corridors wound in and out around the natural stone pillars. The warm wall bewildered her: under the blue smokeless torches it shone purple and black and it seemed to get lower as she went on. When she came at last to a place where it looped over itself, two great cylinders crossing, she pulled up short, stiffening.

A soft voice spoke in her ear. "You can climb over here, my lady. The center is just beyond."

Gingerly, she put a foot on the lower curve. The roughness gave her fingerholds and toeholds to boost herself up, and she was able to reach the top and sit astride it. Breathless, she twisted to see the other side.

"*No.* Oh, no."

She shut her eyes a moment, turning away. The labyrinth

was a serpent. An enormous serpent, far too big to be able to leave the cavern. Its loops and whorls, weaving in and out among the pillars like a Celtic knot, formed a living maze.

Had formed a living maze. It was dead now. Its eyes, like great slabs of obsidian, were milky and glazed. A little blood, black in the torchlight, ran out of its forehead between them and pooled on the floor. A slim figure draped in a blue cloak was standing nearby.

"Go." She hissed the word and made the flinging gesture the guard had used to launch the serpent. She had almost gotten it killed once before; that was one thing which must not happen now.

"For help?"

"Yes, yes, if you like. Just *go.*" To her enormous relief it obeyed, gyring away.

Crouching low over the dead Guardian's back, she stared down at the figure. It—he—was standing in what appeared to be the very center of the chamber, within a ring of low blue flames which burned like Janie's salt circle at home.

Wards, thought Alys. And he's turned them off. The man's head was bowed slightly over a pedestal which rose from the floor and seemed to have been carved out of the raw granite like the pillars. On top of the pedestal was an ivory casket. She saw the glint of silver in one of the man's hands, the flash of gold in the other.

Scarcely breathing, she measured the distance between herself and him. Could she slip down and make it to the central island without being heard? Could she cross the ring and stab before he sensed her and turned? Agonizing seconds dragged by as she debated until something inside her began to laugh grimly.

Not in the back.

She slid down the warm curving wall to land on her feet. Slowly, without a sound, she walked to the edge of the fire.

"Merlin."

He turned around.

Alys drew her breath in sharply. She knew what he looked like; the fragments of dreams told her that. And she recognized the face she'd seen above the nest of wires in Morgana's visioning sphere. But she was still startled—wonderstruck—as she had been when she'd first seen Elwyn. He might be only half Quislai but his beauty was still unearthly. His hair was Elwyn's color and his eyes—

His eyes. They were silver, too, but so dilated it was like looking into void.

Something that flashed gold hit the ground at his feet. Something glinting silver was raised in salute.

Settling her jaw, Alys lifted her own sword, imitating the gesture.

▼　▼　▼

A winged form whiplashed out of the mist above Charles's head.

"Wait! Where's Alys?"

The serpent paused in its flight. "She is in the Serpent's Lair, preparing for battle. She has sent me to find aid . . ."

"What's she battling? The Serpent?"

There was a shocked hiss. "Of course not. It is a sorcerer

I have never seen. He has great power, but the Lady Alys—"

"—has gone crazy! She can't fight magic! Come on— we've got to get somebody who can."

Claudia huddled against the wall as he left, eyes shut, arms locked around Benjamin. She wished, more than anything in the world, even more than she wished to be home, or to be with her mother, or to be in bed realizing that this was all a dream, that Benjamin was the vixen. The vixen always took care of her, protected her, told her what to do. The vixen would tell her what to do now.

Outside the great dome of the white room, violence raged unabated. Shadows loomed out of the mist, the ground shuddered, and the dull rumble of thunder was a continuous background to sudden sharp cries and explosions. Now, above it all, rose the *Fava-se-rá* of the Wild Hunt.

Claudia whimpered. The terrifying sound was getting closer and closer. Janie had said not to run from it, but she wanted to run, to get away. She *had* to get away. She couldn't stand it.

What would the vixen say, if she were here?

Get away, then, a dry little voice seemed to say in her mind. *But don't run.*

But Alys had told her to stay—

Alys! Alys doesn't know everything. She didn't know the Hunt was coming.

Claudia hesitated, then stood, Benjamin still locked in her arms. He was stiff and trembling with terror. The sound had paralyzed him, so that even his faint and faltering powers of communication were lost, but his glazed eyes pleaded with her dumbly.

"We're going to walk away, now," she whispered. "Don't be scared. I'll take care of you. You'll be all right."

She kept talking to him as, head down, step by step, she made her way back toward the white room.

▾ ▾ ▾

Merlin came at her with incredible swiftness. As in the mad struggle with the bobcat-thing, rational thought was suspended and her body took over. The sword seemed to help, telling her what to do. She dodged, parried, and blocked—not gracefully, but adequately. The flash of silver and the ring of steel filled the air.

She didn't have a chance, of course. At some deep level she knew this. Not only was she hopelessly outclassed in swordsmanship, but her opponent had all the advantages of strength and reach and weight. And with every stroke of his weapon the Gem shimmered blue. She had no chance at all of winning, and she had no choice but to try.

Soon they were fighting in the loops and curls of the great serpent's body. Alys kept backing up against the coils, which were knee-high at this point. Prompted by some flash of instinct, she turned to jump on the dead Guardian's body and ran up it. In a swirl of blue cloak, Merlin followed.

▾ ▾ ▾

Charles blundered through the mist, shouting. The fight among Thia Pendriel's people and the Council's people had exploded into a panic. High and clear, the hunting call sounded and sorcerei of both sides ran.

The serpent dipped and wheeled above, guided perhaps by some instinct Charles did not have. He managed to keep it in sight until it dropped suddenly with a hiss of triumph.

"Janie!" She was right in the midst of it, purple eyes blazing. The *Fava-se-rá* sounded again, and she whirled and shouted something to someone.

He grabbed her and whirled her back around. "Janie! Alys is in trouble. You've got to help!"

Adults, grown-ups, were running with the hunters behind them. Charles beat down the panic that washed over him.

"I can't! The Wild Hunt is after everyone—not just Thia Pendriel's people, but everyone! Morgana needs me!"

"*Alys* needs you!" He shook her. "Janie, I think it's Merlin she's fighting—"

Janie cast one agonized look toward a pocket of mist flaming with gold light. Then she spun back.

"Where is she?"

"This way!"

They followed the serpent. At the door, Charles stopped. "*Where's Claudia?*"

They stared at each other. Then Charles gave her a shove. "You go on. I'll find her."

"Don't *run!*" He heard her voice distantly, and shuddered. It was hard, but he no longer felt the urge as strongly as he had before. As he began stumbling through the mist again, some great dark shape leapt over him to land in front. He flinched back automatically, ducking away. Silvery laughter made him fling his head back in surprise.

"Now *this*," said a voice like bells and birdsong, "is fun."

▼ ▼ ▼

Alys stood on the huge, flat head of the serpent. Behind her was nothing but air. Merlin was in front.

So swiftly that she did not see how it happened, the

sorcerer's blade darted at her with a curious twist. The Gem flashed blindingly blue. Her own weapon rippled and seemed to melt into his like quicksilver, dissolving from her grip. She stared stupidly at her empty hand, unable to accept for a moment that Caliborn was gone. Like that, so easily. Then her foot, groping behind her, found empty space, and she jumped backward into it, spinning as she fell.

She hit the ground and came up running. Merlin's blue cape shimmered about him as he dropped. Once again she was backing up, and this time what she came against was the circle of flame. She jumped it and faced him. He was there at once, and the flames blazed up suddenly, encircling them, trapping her. As she turned frantically, seeking escape, her leg twisted under her and she fell.

The next instant he was above her, and she was gazing up into that beautiful, eerily familiar face. Once she looked into his eyes she could not look away. Dilated, they were black and endless with a tiny distant flame burning somewhere within. The room sped away from her. Nothing existed except herself and Merlin and spinning darkness.

▼ ▼ ▼

Janie took two running steps and leaped at the great bulk of the Guardian, the rough scales scraping her hands painfully. Virtue wand tucked into her belt, serpent twined about her neck, she heaved herself up, then half slid, half fell down the other side. From here she could see Alys cross the ring and turn, at bay. She reached the circle just as it exploded up in a conflagration. She gave back, then grabbed at the serpent.

"No! Those wards are killing strength, and you couldn't save her anyway."

"Then, my lady Janie, use your magic—"

"Against a Gem? No magic will help now. Just be quiet!" Through the flames, she saw Alys try to dodge away from the sorcerer, saw her fall heavily and land hard. Janie, released from agonized thought, dragged in a breath, eyes widening. One chance. There was one chance. She plunged a hand into her pocket and drew the sprig of Worldleaf out. Crushing it, she threw it into the heart of the fire. As the pungent, stinging scent rose, she whispered, "Alys, remember. Merlin, remember. *Remember . . .*"

▾ ▾ ▾

Above Alys, Merlin's sword was a pure line of light, and she was falling endlessly into those endless eyes. And then everything changed.

An odor, sharp and distinctive, filled the air. It was spicy and penetrating, and it seemed to shatter some barrier in her head, sweeping away all the darkness and the clouds and the confusion. In this new clarity she heard a voice, at first far away, but getting stronger.

Remember. *Remember . . .*

A great tide of understanding flooded through her and she gasped aloud. Then, slowly, she sat up. The fear was gone. She felt only great astonishment and awe.

The sorcerer had turned sharply toward the origin of the scent to stare at Janie through the flames. Then, as the smoke wafted around him, his head jerked back, his eyes suddenly fixed on nothing.

Alys stood up.

Merlin turned, first his head, then his body, to face her. She remained quite still and met his gaze directly.

"Merlin," she said softly, in a voice of discovery, of wonder. And she held out her hands to him.

They stood like that, eyes locked, for some endless time while the fire leaped and danced about them. Then the sorcerer smiled, a strange and beautiful smile. With an easy gesture he shrugged off his azure cape and placed the sword of Arthur across it.

Then he laid it in her outstretched arms.

The Weerul Council

They faced each other at last. The gaudy trappings of fog were a curiously appropriate background. They had always been at opposite ends of the spectrum, Morgana thought.

The Ice Silver had been raised against her before. So, for that matter, had Heart of Valor. But not together. Although Feathered Serpents winged toward her, although the Archon and his councillors closed in, she knew that Thia Pendriel could kill her before being taken.

Then she heard the *Fava-se-rá.*

Thia Pendriel jerked toward it, caught off guard. The only terror the sound ever held for Morgana was the fear of being tempted to join it, and there was no danger of that now. She attacked without hesitation, throwing a spell of entrapment. After that the struggle was sharp, but there could be only one ending. When it was over, the red Gem lay on the ground between them. And Thia Pendriel, ragged and proud and hating, lay a little distance from it, waiting for Morgana to take the Ice Silver, too. Waiting for the Archon and his folk to arrive.

The hunting call sounded nearer. Thia Pendriel stiffened, shuddering, showing the whites of her eyes. All at once she was fighting again. "Release me!"

Morgana shook her head, but she was tired. She felt the

binding spell break, crumbling under the impact of the Ice Silver's desperation.

"Pendriel, no!" Magic exhausted, Morgana simply tried physically to restrain her. But the councillor's terror gave her strength. She had only one thought: escape.

As the dark shapes swept around Morgana, leaped above her, she saw it was too late. The tall figure had disappeared into the fog, running. The call rang high and clear.

Morgana picked up Heart of Valor.

▾ ▾ ▾

Alys watched the golden tunnel of the portal fade and wink out. He'd left without once saying a word to her. And she hadn't tried to stop him leaving.

A soft sound like a sigh caught her attention. It was the ring of flames, dying down to a flicker. Janie stepped over it; the serpent swooped in to drape around Alys's neck. Together, silently, they turned to the ivory casket on the pedestal.

It was carved with battle scenes and inscriptions. Carefully placing the cloak and sword on the ground, Alys took the upturned golden hasp between thumb and forefinger.

The lid lifted easily. Inside, three stones lay on a field of velvety darkness. It was not cloth. When Alys tried to touch it, her fingers dipped into the dark like water, but she could not feel anything but a slight coolness.

The first Gem fit smoothly into her palm. It was pear-shaped and opaque, forest green swirled with deep blue.

"Rill in the Lea," said Janie.

The second was amethyst, like a chunk of pansy-colored rock candy. "Twilight."

Janie reached for the last, a lump of translucent amber. "And Keep Thee Well." She replaced it. "All here. The three Gems of the rebel councillors."

"And Mirror of Heaven." Alys looked down at the clear blue stone in the pommel of Merlin's sword—her sword. She shut the lid of the casket with a click. When she tried it again it would not open.

"Well," said Janie. "That's that."

Alys found herself gazing again in the direction of the vanished portal. She shook her head hard, then turned back to Janie.

"Janie. I—"

In the blue light Janie's eyes were the color of the pansy-colored Gem. "You're welcome," she said solemnly, and smiled. Alys smiled back and they stood just like that for a moment. Then Alys bundled the cloak and the sword together.

"We'd better get back up there. Anything could be happening."

▼ ▼ ▼

But when they arrived, the battle seemed to be over. The Council chamber was not damaged, but where once there had been tranquility, now there was the stunned aftermath of Chaos. Councillors were scattered about the room, their robes bright splashes against the marble; serpents wheeled continuously in the air. Standing in the doorway, trying to take it all in, Alys saw Morgana and the Archon striding toward them. Claudia was with them, clutching—no, *cradling*—something in her arms. Alys and Janie ran.

"Claudia, where's Charles?"

"I don't know. He left—"

Morgana, reaching them, broke in. Her dark cloud of hair was more unruly than ever, but her voice was steady. "He is in no danger right now, Alys. You need not worry over him. Nor over Thia Pendriel. That has been taken care of."

"All right," said Alys. Wrapped in her new serenity, she was willing to trust Morgana's word with her mind as well as her heart. "Are *you* okay?" she asked Claudia.

Claudia nodded, chin bumping Benjamin. She didn't say anything else, but her blue eyes were dry and almost calm.

"You're brave, you know that?"

"Of course," said Claudia, the stern look coming over her face again.

Morgana spoke quietly. "Where have you been?"

Alys started, remembering. "In the Lair. Fighting Merlin—" She would have gone on, but the Archon interrupted.

"Merlin! Then it *was* true. . . ." He stopped. Suddenly the unlined face looked much older, the hand raised toward Alys trembled. "The Gems."

"They're safe," said Alys. "The Guardian—I'm afraid it's dead. But the Gems are all safe."

Less haggard, the Archon turned aside and spoke to a flying serpent. It and several others departed.

Morgana was studying Alys's face intently. "I am glad," she said, simply. "And surprised—but not astonished."

The Archon had turned back to them. "Morgana, *I* am surprised by all that has passed this night. Clearly, the Council has been blind and mistaken, but I would know the whole story. Can you bring order to this confusion?"

Morgana's eyes were still on Alys. "I might—but I think

it would be better for you and your Council to hear it from these primitives. You may be more surprised yet before they are done."

The Archon lifted his brows, then, after a pause, inclined his head.

"Let it be so, then." Chairs were found and set up on the dais for Alys and Janie and Claudia. Morgana refused one. As the sorcerei took their own places Alys noted that there were only six councillors now. The dark man and Magistress Zoe were gone.

In a few minutes the room had settled into stillness. Morgana broke the silence of the tableau.

"Janie, will you do the honors? Or Alys?"

"Not me." Although Alys was no longer afraid of the councillors—at the moment she was not afraid of anything—she knew she was out of her depth. "I don't understand most of it myself. Janie's the smart one. If she has the answers I'd like to hear them as much as anyone."

Janie bowed her head, looking demure. But when she raised it again, she was serious.

"If I do have any answers it's only because I've just figured them out." She paused a moment as if to gather her thoughts, and Claudia got up and sat in Alys's lap. Alys, feeling quite comfortable with this, rocked her.

"I'll start," said Janie, turning to include the Council, but ending by addressing Alys, "with the most basic question of all, the one you asked in the beginning. What did Thia Pendriel want from our world?

"It wasn't Heart of Valor. She could easily have escaped with that back to Findahl before the mirrors were broken.

But she chose to stay. So there was something else she wanted.

"It wasn't power over our world: she didn't want to rule a planet of animals. It wasn't revenge on Morgana: she could have taken that right away. It was something she couldn't do that night, something she had to *wait* for."

"Mirror of Heaven," said Alys, but a little doubtfully.

"Yes, she needed that. But, more important, she needed *Merlin.*"

There was a responsive stir among the councillors. "Once again," said the Archon, "it would appear we have been deceived. Merlin has long been thought dead, and Mirror of Heaven lost."

"Neither. Morgana put Merlin under a spell of sleep, sealed in a hidden place in our world. He should have stayed there forever, because she used Mirror of Heaven to seal it, before putting that in with him, too. Nothing could break through the seal of a Gem—except a Gem."

"Like Heart of Valor. Which Thia Pendriel had," said Alys, in rising excitement.

"True, with Heart of Valor she could have done it, as long as Morgana didn't manage to stop her. But the seal could only be broken on the same day it was cast, which was May Day. Beltane, the festival of the spring. She knew Morgana would be most on her guard on that day. As for how she actually managed to get around her . . ." Janie frowned slightly and looked questioningly at the little sorceress. "She woke him up even before you arrived?"

"Yes." Morgana's lips were tight, her voice flat with self-disgust. "She knew I would come in good time before Beltane to defend the place. And so I did, setting strong wards about it. But, though she was not able to release Merlin before Beltane, she had used her Gem to awaken him. He would have been dull and sluggish at first, I imagine, but soon he began to remember how to wield Mirror of Heaven. I should have recognized the signs of its rousing."

"All those things happening in the sky," said Alys, eyes widening. "Mirror of *Heaven.* Rainbows and rings around the sun and the aurora . . ."

"Yes," said Janie. "That was Merlin. Still half-asleep and just reaching out to the Gem again, probably. But he woke up fully by Beltane. And at the stroke of midnight Morgana was there waiting, prepared for an attack on the wards from the outside. But Merlin and the tree were *inside* with her. When he used Mirror of Heaven to break out he took her completely by surprise.

"Fortunately, the wards collapsed on her, and there was nothing more he could do to her. Besides, he had to cast a portal right away to get to Thia Pendriel and the Passage."

"But why?" said Alys. "Why was he helping Thia Pendriel? He'd never been on her side before."

Janie looked mildly impatient. "He wasn't so much *for her* as *against Morgana.* And I imagine his cooperation was the price Thia Pendriel demanded for letting him out. Because he was absolutely essential to her plans. Which brings us back to the original question: what did Thia Pendriel want?"

Alys tipped her head in the direction of the Lair. "Those other three Gems? The ones the serpent was guarding?"

"Yes, yes, but you're still thinking too small. She didn't want just three Gems, or four, or five. She wanted all twelve.

She *needed* all twelve. Because she wanted to remake the Black Staff—"

"—of Darion Beldar!" Alys stared at Janie, her mouth dropping open. "But how could she? All the other Gems were destroyed!"

"Not destroyed. Lost. Forgotten. Think about it, Alys. The old councillors, the ones who fought the rebels during the Thousand Years' War, knew they had to get rid of the nine Gems they still had so the rebels wouldn't get them. So they put them in the one place the rebels would never find them, the one place the sorcerei could never go. Or at least not and stay sane. They hid them in Chaotic Zones.

"I began to wonder about that when I knew Cadal Forge had found Heart of Valor in a Chaotic Zone. How he survived I don't know. Maybe he was never sane in the first place. All he saw in Heart of Valor was the perfect means to take his revenge on our world. It didn't occur to him to wonder what it was doing there.

"But it occurred to Thia Pendriel when she heard about it—and she did hear, because he told her. She also knew that long ago Merlin had had a Gem. And where had he gotten it? He said he'd found it lying around while he was wandering. Which sounds like a joke, until you consider the kind of places he was likely to wander into. Chaotic Zones. He ran with the Quislais, and even followed them there.

"So. Thia Pendriel figured out the connection. And that was when she realized she could have all the Gems. Only she couldn't get to them herself, and no full Quislai would ever fall in with her plans. They wouldn't be interested. But *Merlin . . .*

214

"He was perfect. He hated Morgana. He had a grudge against the Council. And he could be bribed with his freedom. Of course, she wanted Mirror of Heaven too, but she didn't tell him that.

"And there you have it. She intended to bring Merlin back to Findahl, have him steal the three Gems in the Lair while she continued to deceive the Council, and then gather the other Gems one by one. And when she had them all . . ." Janie spread out her hands in a wry shrug. "What's better than a Gold Staff? A Black Staff. The only Black Staff. She would have more power than all the rest of the Council put together."

There was a soft release of breath. Alys looked over to see the Archon shaking his head slowly. "I grieve for her," he said. "She had great gifts. She chose to misuse them."

"She *had*? Is she—" Alys hesitated.

It was Morgana who answered. "The Wild Hunt took her." At Alys's expression she added, "It was her choice. And . . . I think . . . for the best. She would have hated imprisonment and ignominy."

Alys considered this. She had feared Thia Pendriel; probably even hated her. But there had been a magnificence about the woman. She thought she understood.

The Archon spoke quietly. "So Heart of Valor is safe at last. And yet Mirror of Heaven is not. We have traded one enemy with a Gem for another."

Alys hesitated. Then, sliding Claudia off her lap, she bent to pick up the bundle.

She looked up to meet the Archon's eyes.

"I don't know if Merlin is your enemy or not," she said,

"but he doesn't have a Gem. He gave it to me."

In the utter silence that followed she unfolded the cloak. Blue fire blazed up at her.

The Archon had come to his feet. His hand reached toward it, then stopped. His dark eyes were on Alys's face.

"He gave it . . . to you. Why?"

Alys opened her mouth and shut it again. She appealed to Janie.

"Well, now," said Janie, half smiling. "I think perhaps she reminded him of someone he knew once. There was . . . a family resemblance."

"It does not," Morgana added steadily to the Archon, "belong to the Council. Heart of Valor has been passed from one thief to another, and can be said to have no owner. The three Gems in the Lair have always been the Council's by right. But this one was found by Merlin and given by him to a human. Now it has been restored to that human's descendant. It is not yours to take.

"But," Morgana said, turning to Alys, "it is yours to give. No one here can compel you, but I would advise you to leave it here in the Wildworld. It has brought sorrow before. And only the sorcerei can hold it harmless."

Once again Alys found herself hesitating. She looked down at the Gem shining as blue as Claudia's eyes, and up into the purple eyes beside her.

"Then I'll give it to a sorceress," she said, and laid it in Janie's arms.

For a moment, as Janie looked down at it, the mad-scientist expression flashed across her face. She was, Alys knew, envisioning the sort of experimental hypotheses one could test out with a Gem of Power. Then she sighed and smiled at Alys. Rising, she placed it at the Archon's feet.

"Know this. That Mirror of Heaven and Heart of Valor will be held harmless and guarded along with their fellows, until the return of Darion or the end of time." Then, to Alys's astonishment and confusion, the Archon bowed, first to her, and then to Janie and Claudia. Face reddening, Alys bowed awkwardly back. Janie did a much better job, looking graceful and sorcerous even in her torn blue jeans. Claudia cuddled dumbly to Alys and stared.

"Alys Lawschildes, Jane Eleanore, and Claudia Diana of Irenahl, take heed. You and your brother are released from the sentence of death imposed by the Council. While the Passages are open, you have freedom of all the lands of Findahl. Let none of the Wildfolk raise a hand against you. And may there be peace between your people and mine."

He meant between their family—their household—and the Finderlais, Alys thought. Didn't he? There had never been peace between the two races, or at least not since the Golden Age of Findahl.

The Archon's sudden change of expression and Morgana's hiss of breath made her turn around quickly. The outer doorway was crowded full of strange people—and strange things. Silently, without fanfare, the Wild Hunt had returned.

At once every staff in the room was raised—mostly by white-knuckled hands, Alys noted. But the electric tension and the predatory aura of the hunters had disappeared. They now seemed merely very beautiful and very strange.

To her shock, she recognized the strange and beautiful young man seated on the lead animal. Elwyn was seated behind him. His shirt was in ribbons.

"Charles. What happened?"

He dismounted and came to the dais, the rest of the group trailing. "Fell in a bramblebush chasing Thia Pendriel. Got *her* out, though." He jerked his head toward Elwyn with some pride. Then he laughed.

The laugh raised goose bumps on Alys's flesh. "Here. Take it. You must be freezing."

He waved away the cloak. "I'm fine." He laughed again. In this light his eyes seemed more gray than blue—almost silvery.

Distinctly alarmed now, Alys turned to Janie, who was exchanging an expressionless look with Morgana.

"Quite right. It's time to go," Morgana said. "Time for *all* of us," she added, looking at Elwyn.

Elwyn smiled ingenuously. One of the riders' mounts stamped.

Morgana rested her staff against the Archon's chair and moved in smoothly until her face was six inches from Elwyn's.

"Elwyn," she said. *"Now."*

Elwyn let out a gusty sigh, leaned sideways around Morgana to dimple at the Archon, and turned.

Charles turned with her.

"Didn't you hear, Charles? We have to get back," said Alys loudly, seizing his shoulder. "Back home. We all need some rest."

"Yes, and what about 'I guess I'll just stay with my sisters'?" added Janie, grabbing from the other side. "Remember that?"

Slowly, the taut muscles under Alys's fingers loosened. Charles slumped a little. "Oh. Yeah."

Elwyn's move toward him was forestalled by Morgana. "Well, then, good-bye," she said, looking wistful. The effect of which was rather spoiled when, not waiting for a reply from Charles, she lilted off without a backward look. The Wild Hunt followed her.

Morgana was examining Charles's forehead. "I thought I told you to watch out for the signs."

"I did," said Janie defensively. "Things got a little complicated, is all."

"Ah, well. No real harm done—this time. We shall deal with it later. Now we leave."

The Archon bowed once more. "Morgana of Findahl and Irenahl, you are no longer an exile. Go, with the Council's thanks, and return, when you will, with our blessing. The quarrel between us is ended."

▼   ▼   ▼

Walking back down the colonnade of light, Alys felt dreamy. Exhaustion, she thought, seeing the pale green of dawn light the eastern sky.

"What happened to the platinum-plus pigsticker?" said Charles. It was the first thing he'd said since Elwyn left.

"Oh." Alys looked down at her empty hands, flexing them. "Merlin happened."

"And," said Janie, "you left the other with the Council. You could have just let them take Mirror of Heaven out of it, you know."

"I . . . didn't want it." Alys wasn't sure how to explain what she meant. "I'm not very good at hanging on to weapons, anyway," was the best she could do. But Morgana met her eyes with understanding.

"If the need ever arises," said the sorceress, "I will make you another. I hope it will not arise."

Alys nodded. *That* was what she'd meant, exactly.

"Caliborn—it gave me dreams about you," she said, almost shyly, knowing Morgana already knew this. "But how?"

"Where did the last dream end for you?"

Alys cast her mind back. "On the battlefield. When Arthur—when the king—was dying. He gave you the sword and you promised to take care of Guinevere."

"And I kept that promise—and the other, the one I made long before, to his mother. To protect her line, Arthur's line." She added after a moment, "Merlin asked it of me, as well. His last words, actually."

" 'The child . . .' " Alys remembered. "I thought he meant Arthur."

"So did I at the time. But he wasn't rambling. He knew things. Knew, for example, that Arthur's line would continue, and would need help and protection. The little girl I raised in my household, and her child after her, and so on. Even when I renounced sorcery for a time, the spell to keep their descendants close to me endured. I wanted them nearby, just in case. When you took the sword you wakened it once more. It had always kept a rapport between Arthur and me. Now that rapport was transferred to you. But the vixen knew all this; why did she not tell you?"

There was a silence. Then Morgana said, "Where is the vixen?"

The Hodges-Bradley family mentally drew straws, and Alys, of course, lost. She braced herself, and then, as concisely as possible, told Morgana.

It was as bad as she thought. The little sorceress lost all expression on hearing the vixen's speech to Claudia, and in the end she simply said flatly, "I see."

Alys laid a hand on her arm. "Oh, Morgana. I'm sorry."

"So am I," said Morgana. "Especially as she was wrong. She *was* free. Always. But perhaps now she realizes it."

Claudia pulled up. Alys thought she was lagging from tiredness until she saw her face.

"What is it?"

Claudia was looking down at the white shape in her arms. The soft radiance of the pillars reflected iridescently off soft fur.

"Benjamin," Claudia said, "wants to be free, too."

Alys, appalled, knelt before her. "You mean . . ."

"He wants to stay. And I don't blame him. I . . . want him to." She looked up at Morgana. "If he'll be safe."

"As safe as any rabbit ever is," said Morgana, a bit heartlessly, Alys thought. Softening, she added, "The touch of magic in him will be to his advantage."

Claudia slowly crouched down and loosened her arms. At the last moment, she looked wide-eyed at Janie.

"I forgot . . ."

"Oh, don't stop on my account," said Janie hastily. "Believe me, I couldn't agree more."

Claudia let go. Benjamin sat a moment, whiskers twitching. He looked at Claudia and hopped a step away, then another. Then, as she bit her lip and nodded, he hopped straight into the darkness between the columns and disappeared.

Alys put an arm around Claudia's small shoulders, while looking up at Morgana's brooding face. What we need, she thought, is some way to lighten things up around here. A bit desperately she realized she had absolutely no idea how.

She heard Charles's voice behind her.

"I bet," he said deliberately, "that they still have that iguana down at ProPets."

Just as deliberately, Janie smacked him. "You're insufferable. Also disreputable. Look at you. Look at that disgusting T-shirt—"

"What's wrong with it? Just needs a little washing. For that matter, look at *you*. . . ."

They managed to make the squabble last all the way to the Passage.

▾ ▾ ▾

Midsummer Day

It was June 21, the summer solstice. The longest day of the year. Claudia, on her way to Morgana's house, had no time to admire the drowsy beauty of the world around her. Alys's voice on the phone had been imperative. She had interrupted Claudia's reading lesson with the new tutor to summon her.

The back door of Fell Andred stood open. In a corner of the warm kitchen Charles and Janie and Morgana and Alys were bent over something on the floor. The serpent was coiled around Alys's arm. Everyone was smiling.

Claudia edged her way between the bigger bodies, bewildered. Then she gasped aloud. The next instant she was crying.

"Yes, yes," said the vixen, squirming on the nest of soft, old blanket. "That is to say, yes, but not on the little ones. They don't like wet."

"Oh, they're beautiful." Claudia released her stranglehold on the vixen and put out a finger to touch one tiny dark-furred body. She hesitated, eyeing the finger doubtfully. It was grimy.

"Just this once," the vixen said. "Anyone else who tries it, I bite," she added to Charles. Charles leaned against the kitchen wall, grinning.

"Four of them," he said. "One for each of us."

"They're not any of them for you," said Morgana sharply. "They're for themselves."

"All for one and one for all," Claudia babbled, intoxicated by the feel of velvety plush fur under her finger tips. "I'm so glad you decided to come back," she added softly.

"Our den was disturbed," said the vixen. But, Claudia noticed, she did not move away when Morgana scratched behind her neck where the collar once had been, or bite when Morgana gently cupped a palm around the smallest pup.

"That one is Thistle. She'll take after her father, I'm afraid. The others are Berry, Blossom, and Thorn."

Charles looked surprised. "I didn't know you named them. I mean, *you* don't have a name."

"Of course I have a name! Given me by my own mother, which is in the proper scheme of things. I just don't happen to like it."

"What is it?"

The vixen looked long-suffering. Charles joined Claudia on the floor to coax, wheedle, and bribe. Alys and Janie, at Morgana's touch on their shoulders, moved away.

"Have you given any more thought to the Council's proposition?" the sorceress asked as they walked out of the house into the golden stillness of the summer day.

"Yes." The serpent wound up Alys's arm and she rested her cheek against its head for a moment. "And . . . I don't know. Morgana, I do want to help. And there's nothing I'd like better than to be an ambassador for our world. But— well, I don't think I'm right for it."

"You're the best we have."

Alys sighed. "No, you don't understand. It isn't false modesty. It's that I make so many mistakes—and so much of what I do turns out wrong. . . ." She stopped. Morgana was laughing.

"Well, in that, at least, you are like *him*. Like Arthur. He made almost every mistake there is. But for a short time he made people want to work together, to put aside their differences. He made them hope. For him, they tried to be better than they were. Even I tried."

"But—"

"If anything is needed, it is the ability to unite, to forge understanding. That you have. I am not saying this rash plan of the Council's will work. The Wildfolk are wary and suspicious of humans, and humans will be equally suspicious of them. It will not be easy to bring them together. It may not even be possible. Times have changed since the sorcerei were worshiped like gods."

"And I don't think things can ever go back to the way they were."

"With fear on one side and contempt on the other? I hope not. If the breach is to be healed, new ways must be found."

"And remember," put in Janie, "unless you agree, there's no guarantee they'll let the Passage stay open. Which means I'll never get to compete for my staff. Don't you want me to be a sorceress?"

"I think you're mostly there already." Alys turned to Morgana. "I'll do it," she said. "For a year, like you advised me. I'll be proud to." She laughed suddenly. "Look at us.

Claudia's reading, Janie's going to be a real sorceress; I'm going to be—"

"—a hero—"

"Hah. Heroes do things like fight monsters."

"Much better," said Morgana, "to forge alliances and mend bridges. Much harder, too."

"And Charles . . ."

"What about Charles?" The voice came from the doorway. Charles added, to Morgana, "The vixen wants you."

Morgana's movements were always bird-swift, but this time she flew. Alys, catching a glimpse of her face, smiled.

Then she gazed at her brother, lounging against the door-jamb—he did a lot of lounging these days—with a shaft of sunlight illuminating his hair. For a moment he looked quite different to her eyes. Older and wilder and more beautiful. But also sad. Then he grinned and scratched his collarbone and the spell was broken.

"You haven't seen anything of Elwyn lately, have you?" she couldn't help asking.

"Elwyn who? Oh, you mean that nut case with all the hair? No, can't say I have. Can't say I want to, either . . ."

Janie spoke in Alys's ear. "He's got her anklet in his drawer at home. Really. I'm not joking."

Alys pushed aside thoughts of Thomas the Rhymer and Morgana's father and all the other mortals who had fallen in love with Quislais. Charles would be all right, she knew that somehow. Charles, no matter what maelstrom raged around him, would always end up all right.

"I'm going to miss him," she said, as she watched him

sauntering off. She was surprised at how true it was. "I'm going to miss everyone."

"Even me?"

"Especially you. After all, what am I going to do without anybody to argue with?"

Janie looked at her, then away. She cleared her throat, then frowned. "Well, you don't have to go to Findahl for a while yet. In the meantime, how about us doing some more sister things together?"

Alys snorted. "Like what?"

"Oh, I don't know. Slay a few monsters, outwit a few magicians, drain a few Chaotic Zones, negotiate a few treaties . . ."

"And *after* lunch?"

Janie returned the wry grin sweetly. "I'll let you know."

The hero and the sorceress walked back up the path arm in arm.